The Seventh Son of the Seventh Son

By J. D. Harris

Cover design by Bill Womack (lblueyonder.com)

ISBN: 1503343278

ISBN 13: 9781503343276

Library of Congress Control Number: **XXXXX (If applicable)**

LCCN Imprint Name: **City and State (If applicable)**

Thanks

To my wife Cheryl for her undying support and belief in me

To my sister Alice for her encouragement

To Jim Lester for his feedback

Chapter 1

Killian G. O'Rourke was digging potatoes, and the sweat burned his eyes. He blinked three or four times, but that only made it worse. He could taste the salt as he licked the side of his mouth. It was five o'clock, and he had been at it since five that morning. Killian looked down at the dirt under his fingernails. He thought, "There's got to be a better way of making a living than this." As he stood up and stretched his aching back, old man Connery came out and handed him ten shillings for the day's work.

"I'll see you tomorrow, then?" the old man said.

Killian, six foot two, looked down at the man who was barely five feet tall. "Mr. Connery, I sincerely hope you never see me again in your lifetime," he said, hoping the man would take offense and fire him. If he didn't have enough sense to quit on his own, maybe being fired would push him in a direction he hadn't tried before.

Mr. Connery smiled. "I understand how you feel, but if there's a better job or any job other than this one, you should take it," he said, and he walked back to the house. The old man placed his cane carefully as he trod a well-worn path.

It was 1885, and Ireland was having a terrible time feeding its population. There were not enough jobs, and everything seemed worse because Killian's mother had died the year before. His dad was doing all he could do, but the fact was that his dad and his six brothers were working, and there was still not enough to eat.

Killian was tired and smelled of the manure used to fertilize the potatoes. He trudged along with his jacket over his shoulders, his brown brogans kicking up dust in the road. His cap sat on the back of his head, and his red hair waved in the wind. He shuddered at the thought that he would be back in the fields in less than twelve hours. He lived a few miles from the sea in County Cork on the southern coast of Ireland, just outside Queenstown. He walked along thinking that there had to be a better life than this.

When he went into a house that looked like all the other houses in that part of County Cork, his father looked at him. "Put your wages in the jar. How much did you get?"

"Same as I always get, Papa. You know old man Connery is going to pay me the same, so why do you always ask?"

His father looked up from washing the dishes in a brown, wooden bucket. "I know it's not much, but every bit helps to put food on the table."

After washing his hands, Killian plopped down at the table and thought for a minute. "Why don't you let me go to America? It can't be any worse than this."

His father looked at him with narrowed eyes as he wiped his hands on his apron. "If you go to America, they will make a freak out of you. They will make you look like a circus clown."

"How will they do that? And why are you the only brother who stayed in Ireland? The rest have made their fortunes in America. It seems like you would want to do the same." Killian loved to reread the few letters that his father had received from his six brothers in America. He thought that America must be the greatest escape possible from a backbreaking life of long hours for little pay.

His father looked at him carefully. "My brothers may not be as well off as they let on in their letters. They just want us to think that. The point is, you're not going."

Killian's father walked over and set a bowl of boiled cabbage and potatoes down in front of him. "Go ahead and eat. Your brothers have all finished."

Killian looked at the wooden bowl. The smell of potatoes and cabbage almost made him sick. He had come to hate cabbage and potatoes. Besides porridge and boiled cabbage and potatoes, there was little else to eat. He ate them, though, and looked up at his father. "Papa, would you let me go to the coast and look for a job? If I can't go to America, maybe I can find work unloading ships or something."

His father didn't even look back at him. "Son, I would, but we need the money you bring home every day. We can't do without it."

Killian thought for a moment. "I think it would make things better if I left."

His father stopped doing dishes, and he stood there wearing the same work pants and brogans that they all wore. He turned and looked at his son. "How would your leaving make things better?"

"Well…" Killian paused. "If you consider breakfast, lunch, and dinner, it costs more than what I make to pay for that. I think one less person eating an Irish pound's worth of food would be a savings from that person bringing home ten shillings a day, wouldn't it?"

His father didn't say anything for a while and turned back to washing the dishes. He finally looked at his son again. "If I let you go to Queenstown, will you promise me you will send money home and not try to buy passage to America?"

"Oh, yes, Papa. I certainly would. When can I go?" His heart was racing at the thought of doing anything besides digging potatoes.

"Do you want to give Mr. Connery notice? You may need the job again someday."

Killian looked up from the disgusting dish he was eating. "No, sir. I don't intend to dig potatoes for Mr. Connery ever again. I'll make my fortune on the coast or die trying."

His father smiled. "At least you have the attitude for it. Go with my blessing."

He jumped up and kissed his father on the cheek. "I'll leave tomorrow morning if that's OK with you." His father nodded, trying not to show his sadness.

Killian was the only child out of seven who had the red hair of his father. He loved his father, but he never felt the connection he had had with his mother. His mother had always told him he was special and that he would realize it someday.

The next morning, he said good-bye to each of his brothers and their wives. He kissed the children, and after his brothers had gone off to work, Killian packed his rucksack with the three outfits of clothes he owned and stuck his brogans in it. He put on his best shirt, pants, and shoes. He wanted to make an impression on the first person he asked for a job. His father gave him two pounds. "Here, this will hold you until you can make some money."

"Thanks, Papa. I'll make you proud." His father turned and went back into the house.

He started on the three-hour walk to Queenstown. The sadness of leaving his family tempered his excitement at escaping that barren existence. Halfway there, the sun was getting warmer, and he could smell the salt air from the sea now.

About that time, a horse and cart came by, and the driver, an old man in a pale-green suit, stopped. "Where you headed, young man?"

"To the coast. Are you going that way?"

"Oh yes, be getting in and I'll give you a ride."

Killian was grateful for the ride; he was already tired. He closed his eyes as the man tried to engage him in conversation. Killian answered him, but kept his eyes closed, dreaming about carrying large boxes off a ship. The sun was hot on his face.

When they reached Queenstown and, the cart came to a creaking stop on a busy street. The city hustled and bustled around them. Merchants displaying their wares and shoppers carefully looked them over. Horse-drawn vehicles rattled up and down the cobblestone street.

Killian gave his thanks to the man and walked toward the dock area, hoping to get a job there. As he crossed a busy street in front of a row of shops, he saw a horse and carriage coming at a gallop. He looked to see how far it was to the opposite curb, and that's when he saw a ball roll into the street from the other side. A boy about five or six years old was chasing it.

Killian threw his rucksack off his shoulders, ran for the boy, and grabbed him, pushing him out of the way of the galloping horses. It was so close that one of the horse's legs hit his foot as he dove in front in front of the team. Killian turned in midair so he would land on his back and not on the boy. He slid to the curb. The boy's ball lay in the street, deflated by the runaway horses. A man and a hysterical woman ran over and picked the crying boy up. They put him on the sidewalk and checked to see if he was all right. An elderly man walking with a cane approached Killian with tears in his eyes. "I want to thank you for saving my grandson's life."

"That's OK," Killian said, looking across the street at his rucksack just as a man in a cart picked it up and drove off at a run. "Hey! That's my sack—bring it back!"

The man in the cart looked back and waved, smiling, but kept going. The older man was standing there looking at Killian. "It seems you have ruined your clothes."

Killian looked down and saw that his shirt was torn at the shoulder and the back pocket of his pants was ripped. His heart sank. What bad luck!

"This is wonderful. My extra clothes get stolen, and my best clothes get torn. Now I will never get a job." He couldn't believe that his new life was starting so badly."

The old man, who was dressed in a fine, expensive suit, looked at Killian with aged eyes. "What kind of job are you looking for?"

Killian looked down the street where the cart had gone. "One where I can make enough money for a ticket to America." He continued to look at his clothes. He was a little surprised by his own revelation that he was seeking a way to America.

The old man stuck out his hand. "My name is Carlton Smyth. Come with me. I think we can do something about this."

He followed Mr. Smyth down the street, and they turned into an expensive men's clothing store. They walked through the green door of heavy oak and entered a room with coats, trousers, and shirts of all sizes and colors. It smelled like new clothes.

The clerk, obviously greeting an old customer, said, "Good day, Mr. Smyth. How are we today?"

"Fine, Phillip. I need this man outfitted in four sets of clothes and send me the bill."

The man nodded. "Very good, sir."

He took Killian over to a rack of pants and held up a pair. "How about these?"

Carlton nodded. "That'll be fine."

Killian looked at the fine dress pants. "Wait a minute, sir. I appreciate what you are doing, but I need work clothes to get a job." He wished he had such fine clothes, but he knew they weren't practical.

Carlton shook his head. "You saved my grandson's life. I am forever indebted to you. These clothes are what you need to get on a ship to America. I am going to replace your clothes that were stolen, along with the ones that were damaged, and buy you a ticket to America." To the clerk, he added, "Continue please." The clerk brought out more clothes as Killian stood there in amazement.

Killian walked out in a new suit, carrying a new suitcase with three sets of clothes in it, including underwear, socks, and an extra pair of shoes. Carlton slowly walked him down to the dock and purchased a ticket for him. He looked at Killian. "You're in luck. The ship sails today. Here's ten dollars in US money. You will need it when you get there." Then he smiled at Killian.

Killian shook the old man's hand, still in disbelief. "I don't know how to thank you for what you've done."

Carlton responded, "It is I who should be thanking you, and I know how to do that. Enjoy your trip to America. Come back to Ireland when you get rich and famous. We need fine young men such as you." Killian admired the man's willingness to share his wealth and thought that was something he would certainly do when he made his fortune.

Carlton walked away, and Killian headed for the ship. He passed a market that had cheese and biscuits for sale, and he bought two pounds' worth, thinking it would feed him on the ship. After boarding the ship, he would have no more use for the pound notes his father had given him. He took the food to the ship and boarded it. He had never seen a ship that size up close. It had a hull of steel, it was six stories high, and it had a new coat of gray paint that shone in the sun. He was shown to a room that was about eight feet by ten feet. It had a bed, a washbasin, and a toilet. He looked at the man in a uniform who had led the way and admired his blue, double-breasted coat over white pants. Even the man's shoes were white without a scuff on them. Not even a layer of dust.

"Are you sure this is where I'm supposed to be?" Killian had never expected to have a room, much less a private room.

The man looked at Killian's ticket as he gave it back to him. "That's what your ticket says." Killian acknowledged him with a nod, went in, and shut the door, grateful for such a nice room. He had heard all kinds of stories about sitting in steerage, where a lot of people were crowded into a big room.

That night, he ate some of his cheese and biscuits. They tasted so much better than cabbage and potatoes. He walked around the ship, sight-seeing, for the next three days. After a few days, eating the biscuits for three meals a day was getting kind of old. The cheese finally went bad, and he threw it and the stale biscuits out. That evening, he was walking around the ship and he passed a dining room. Wonderful smells of all kinds of food wafted out. He had only dreamed of such food. He asked a uniformed man how much it cost to eat in there. The man asked to see his ticket, so Killian produced it, and the man looked at it. "The food costs you nothing. It's covered in the cost of the ticket. Would you like to be seated?"

Killian couldn't believe his luck. New clothes, passage to America, and free food. He was a little perturbed at himself for wasting three days on cheese and biscuits. He went in and was shown a menu, and he ordered vegetables and lamb, a staple in Ireland that he seldom got to taste. He sat at a table with a white cloth; the glasses sparkled, as did the silverware. The waiters were in white, crisp uniforms with white gloves. The aroma of the food of nearby patrons smelled so good it made his stomach growl. A server brought some bread and butter, and the warm bread seemed to melt in his mouth. The lamb was the best he had ever tasted, and the vegetables balanced out a perfect meal. Afterward, he had a bowl of bread pudding.

This was something he had heard about but never tasted. He had never eaten so well in his entire life. He thought to himself, "If America is anything like this, I will have to write Papa and my brothers."

Chapter 2

The voyage was uneventful because the weather was good the whole trip. He met some Irish people leaving Ireland for America, as he was, and he met Americans who were going back home. When they docked at Ellis Island in New York, it took seven hours for Killian to process through. He seemed to take three steps, wait thirty minutes, and then take three more steps and wait again. They asked the same few questions in several different ways, and he wondered why. He signed the last piece of paper and finally walked out on the street after the ferry ride to the mainland, but had no idea which way to go. As he started down the street, he heard two men talking with Irish brogues.

He walked up to them. "Excuse me. I just got off the ship. Can you tell me if there is an Irish community about?"

One pointed. "You head down this way, turn left at Marlbury Street. Then go about twenty blocks, and you will hear the familiar."

Killian looked in that direction. "What's a block?"

The man laughed. "From one street corner to the next is a block." Killian thanked him and started walking. He found Marlbury Street, turned, and started down it. He was more excited than ever.

He had walked about eighteen blocks when three young men about his age came out of an alleyway in front of him. One of them said, "I don't recognize you. Are you new to the neighborhood?" The boys were wearing overalls and striped T-shirts. They wore old, unpolished shoes, and each boy looked as if he needed a haircut.

Killian looked them over. "I don't live here. I'm just passing through."

"Oh no, sounds like another Irish hooligan. You don't pass through our neighborhood unless you get permission, and then only if you pay the proper toll. Isn't that right, boys?" The other two nodded their heads.

Killian shrugged. "I'm sorry, but I didn't see a sign anywhere, and I don't have any money for a toll." He figured he might have to fight his way out of this and dreaded messing up a good set of clothes.

The first boy stepped up close to Killian. "Then you must take a beating." The other two punched their hands with their fists.

Killian gave a look of resignation. "Well, if I must, I must, I suppose," he said. He stood there as if he were ready to be punched in the face. The three boys surrounded him; when the first one drew back his fist, Killian threw his suitcase at him. "Hold this." As the boy caught the suitcase, Killian hit him in the mouth. He turned quickly and hit the second boy in the right eye, just as the third landed a fist to Killian's left eye. The other two went down with the punches, and the third looked down in surprise to see his two friends bleeding. Before he could look back, Killian nailed him right in the nose. He too started gushing blood. He backed away from Killian, stumbled, and fell. Killian saw that none of them was getting up, so he picked up his suitcase, turned, and continued his journey. He thought, "Well, that's one advantage to having six brothers and being the youngest." Growing up, he'd had to fight for everything he wanted.

Two blocks away, he heard someone yell, "There he goes! Get him!"

When he looked back, he saw a police officer running toward him, followed by the three boys. He turned at the next street, trying to find a hiding place. He didn't fancy going to jail his first day in America. He ran past about six houses and knew they would be at the corner soon, so he ran up a driveway. As he got to the backyard, there was a woman hanging laundry on the line. She was as tall as any woman he had ever seen. She had on a simple print housedress with a pair of black lace-up shoes. She was portly, but she carried the weight well.

She put her hands on her hips. "Who are ye, and where do ya think you're going?"

He was so glad to hear the Irish accent. "There's a peeler and three thugs after me because I'm Irish."

"Oh there is, is there? Go in the house, and I'll handle this."

He walked into the house and looked out the side window. He saw the woman walk to the front. The police officer and the three boys got there at the same time. The police officer stopped. "Have you seen an Irish hooligan run through here, ma'am?"

She put both hands on her hips. "So, he's a hooligan because he's Irish, eh? Well, I'm Irish. Do you want to try and arrest me?" She walked toward the officer. "And didja know that when you turned the corner back there, you were in an Irish neighborhood?"

The officer looked around, and there were people standing on their stoops with their hands on their hips. The cop and the boys looked worried.

The woman stepped closer to the four of them. "Now, we wouldn't want to do anything illegal, so let's ask the policeman what he would like to do."

The cop smiled. "Very good. Now, I—"

"Shut up," she interrupted him. "Officer Murphy, can you help settle this dispute?" Killian leaned against the glass to see another police officer step up. He was about a foot taller than the first.

"Now what seems to be the problem here, Fritz?" Officer Murphy asked.

The woman looked at Fritz. "They are looking for an Irish hooligan, the man says."

Murphy looked shocked. "Irish hooligans? Irish hooligans? I've not seen any Irish hooligans. What did he do?"

Fritz gulped. "He pounded on these two, uh three boys, and bloodied all three of them."

Murphy looked confused. "You mean one Irish hooligan bloodied three English shits? I call that a fair fight where I come from. How about you, Mrs. O'Malley?"

"Aye, a fair fight is what it sounds like to me. How about you, Officer Fritz?"

Officer Fritz turned and started shooing the boys with his hand and his baton back down the street.

Murphy yelled after the retreating cop. "And if I ever need you on my beat again, Fritz, I'll be sure and holler for you."

The four hurried away quickly.

Mrs. O'Malley turned, walked around the house, and came in the back door. "Those roughens won't be bothering you again, I can assure you of that. Did they give ya the black eye?"

Killian nodded, suddenly feeling the pain in his swelling eye.

"Now, where are you coming from, and where are you going?"

"I come from Ireland to try to find relatives in this country."

"Fresh from Ireland, are ye? Well, where did you live in Ireland?"

"We have a small farm on the southern coast of County Cork, in Queenstown."

"Cork, I left there me self some years ago. Didja know Harry and Glenda Albright?"

"No ma'am, but I knew Horace Albright. He lived on the next farm from us."

"Horace? 'Tis his brother, for sure. Dear friends of mine many years ago. Now what is your name, and who are ye looking for?"

"My name is Killian G. O'Rourke, and I'm looking for my six uncles and their families."

"O'Rourke, huh? I think Mildred Brown was an O'Rourke before she married. We'll have to visit her after I fix you something to eat."

Even though he was starving, Killian looked at the woman. "I don't want to put you out."

"My name is Gwynn O'Malley, and 'tis no trouble at all. My husband is working the night shift at the boiler factory, and he won't be home until the wee hours of the morning. Now sit yourself down here."

She made him a supper of pork chops, potatoes, and lima beans with homemade bread. He had never had pork chops before or lima beans, and the potatoes were fried. After they ate, Gwynn got her brown, hand-knitted shawl and put it on.

"Follow me," she said, leading him out the door.

Killian followed her. They turned left, walked past about ten houses, and knocked on a door. A woman, about the age of Mrs. O'Malley, came to the door.

Gwynn smiled real big. "Mildred, darling, how are ye today?"

"Fit as a fiddle, Gwynn. Please come in."

"Mildred, this is Killian G. O'Rourke, and he's looking for family in the States. He's fresh from Ireland, ya know."

Mildred put her hands to her face. "Oh, how I miss Ireland. Now Killian, what does the G stand for?"

Killian looked back at her sheepishly. "I'd rather not say, ma'am, if you don't mind."

The two women crossed their arms over their chests and just stared at him. He knew he had better not cross these two. "It stands for Gilhooley. It was my mother's maiden name. My father wanted to make sure I was called Killian, so he stuck me with a name that was sure to get me in a fight if I used it."

The two women broke up laughing. Gwynn looked at Mildred. "When I was a little girl, me best friend was Margaret Gilhooley."

Killian looked at her, astonished. "My mother's name was Margaret."

"You said was?"

Killian nodded. "She passed away about a year ago."

Gwynn lowered her head. "I'm so sorry."

Mildred looked at his swollen eye. "Who gave the eye to you?"

Killian touched his sore eye and looked back at Mildred. "Nobody gave it to me; I fought for it."

Gwynn and Mildred laughed again.

"Now, Mildred, do you know any O'Rourkes anywhere?"

She put her hand on her chin. "Well now, all the O'Rourkes I knew left New York to settle land in East Tennessee somewhere. Knoxville, I think it was. Around this neighborhood, you see a lot of orange, us being Protestants and all. Most of the Protestants went to either Syracuse or Knoxville. Either place, you'll see a lot of orange and know you're among good people. Now, I don't know of any O'Rourkes who went to Syracuse. But if you're going to look, Syracuse is a lot closer than Tennessee. Who are you looking for exactly?"

Killian looked at her with some anticipation. "Any of my six uncles or their families."

"Six uncles? I remember a bunch of O'Rourke brothers who went to Tennessee."

"How far is Tennessee?" Killian asked with more anticipation.

"Oh, you would have to walk from one end of Ireland to the other three or four times to get to Tennessee."

Killian looked crestfallen.

Gwynn put her hand on his shoulder. "Did you leave family in Ireland?"

"Yes ma'am. My father and six brothers."

Gwynn and Mildred quickly looked at each other and raised their eyebrows, and then Mildred looked at him. "I thought you said you had six uncles."

Killian looked confused. "I did. Is that a problem?"

"Is your father the seventh brother?"

"Yes, ma'am."

"Are you the youngest of your brothers?"

"Yes, ma'am."

Mildred's eyes seemed to get bigger. "Then you are the seventh son of a seventh son."

"Yes, ma'am, I suppose so. Why?"

"No reason," she said, casting a look at Gwynn. "No reason."

Gwynn looked at Mildred for a few seconds. "Well, we must be going. This young man will be staying with me until we can get him train fare to Tennessee. I'll be in touch, Mildred."

Mildred nodded and gave Gwynn a certain look. Killian and Gwynn got up and walked back to Gwynn's house. "Are ye tired, young man?"

"Yes, ma'am." Killian really began to feel how tired he was.

"Well, let's get you to bed and you get some rest."

She showed him to a bedroom and told him to get in bed, and she showed him the water closet. He undressed and got in bed and went right to sleep. Killian was in a room that had a small bed, a chest for clothes, and a cabinet. There was an oval mirror on the wall. The room was painted beige and had light-brown curtains that matched the bedspread.

Just before he went to sleep, he thought, "I'm really fortunate to have found Mrs. O'Malley. I wonder how I can get to Tennessee." He went to sleep thinking about his papa and wondering if he was going to be mad at him for coming to America.

The next day, there was a knock on the door while Killian was eating breakfast, and Gwynn introduced him to the caller. The woman put down two dollars and left. Soon there was another knock, and the same thing transpired with the money. By the end of the day, so many people had come by that Killian had lost count. There was a big pile of money in a large bowl. Killian looked at the bowl. "Why are all these people coming by and leaving you money?"

"Oh, they're just interested in helping you find your family."

"You mean they are leaving all that money for me?"

"Yes, 'tis true."

Killian frowned. "I don't know what to say. First a man buys me clothes and pays me fare to America and now this."

Gwynn narrowed her eyes. "Why did he do that for ye?"

Killian was deep in thought about all the recent events that had brought him to where he was. "Oh, a horse and carriage almost ran over his grandson, and I pushed the boy out of the way. I ruined the clothes I had on, and my sack was stolen while I was doing it. The man was grateful, so he bought the clothes and the ticket."

"Of course! You saved the child, that's for sure."

The Reverend Michael Beal came by and brought some money from the church fund. Killian was introduced, and the minister looked at him. "'Tis so nice to make your acquaintance. Go with God, young man."

Killian looked lost. "I don't understand why all this is happening. I seem to be having a string of good luck I've never had before in me life. First, new clothes and a trip to America, now money for train fare. I don't know what to think about all this."

Gwynn smiled. "I know you don't, but you will someday. Now we must go and get ye aboard the train to Tennessee." She gathered up the money, counted it, and there was one hundred fifty-five dollars.

Killian looked at her. "Maybe you ought to give some back. I have ten dollars from the man that bought me the clothes and the ticket."

"No, no, young man. This is for you. Please don't disappoint the people who gave it by refusing it."

With that, he took the money. Gwynn put on a hat with a little red daisy sticking up in the front and then her gray coat that almost reached the floor. She looked at him. "Come with me," she said.

He picked up his suitcase full of clean clothes. They walked out the front door to the curb and seemed to be waiting. Soon, a horse and cart stopped. The driver unlatched the door, and it swung open. Gwynn stepped in, and Killian followed.

Killian shut the door, and the cart pulled away. He could hear the wood creak as it turned. The driver wore a worn suit, with a flat hat on his head, and smoked a pipe that smelled bad. He never said a word, but carried himself as if he were on a mission from God.

They turned around in the street and went in the direction the cart had come from, and Killian was glad because they would not pass the alley where the three toughs had attacked him. After a bumpy, forty-five-minute ride in a cart with no springs, they came to the train station. When they got out, Gwynn faced him and took him by the shoulders. Killian was over six feet tall, and at eighteen years old, he wasn't through growing, but he was only slightly taller than Mrs. O'Malley was.

She hugged him. "If ya don't find who you're looking for, come back here. Will ya?"

Killian smiled. "I will never forget the kindness you have done me."

Gwynn looked at him as if she had known him all his life. "That's all I can hope for." She smiled, hugged him again, and got back in the cart. Killian waved as it drove away, and he saw that Mrs. O'Malley had tears in her eyes. He was choked with emotion himself.

24

Chapter 3

He walked to the ticket window. "I would like to get to Knoxville, Tennessee."

The ticket man looked down his nose at Killian and sneered as he said, "If I can do anything to get the Irish out of New York, I'll be glad to help you."

Killian looked back at him showing no fear. "I'd be grateful." He sounded just as condescending. Killian wondered why so many New Yorkers seemed to dislike the Irish.

The man looked at him for a minute. "You'll have to change trains three times, but this will get you there. That'll be seventeen dollars."

Killian gave him the money, and he took the tickets printed in black and green ink that the man shoved under the wire cage. He checked them to make sure they would take him all the way to Tennessee. Then he looked at the ticket agent behind the wire partition. "If you're going to talk like an arse, you had better stay in the cage they've built for ye." He turned and walked away.

He stopped a man in uniform and showed him his ticket, hoping he didn't have to speak for fear of having to defend his Irish accent.

The man pointed down the platform. "Track six and it leaves in a few minutes, so you better hurry."

Killian ran down past the trains sitting still, and he got to track six as the train started to pull out. He ran and jumped on the steps, and the porter took his suitcase for him. He looked at him with a smile, saying "Thanks." He tried to sound as if he had an American accent and vowed to try to lose his native tongue, since it seemed to get him in fights. Besides, he had become an American.

He took his suitcase and went to the middle of the car, where he saw an empty seat. He put his suitcase overhead and sat down. He watched New York roll by, and it reminded him of the poor in Ireland. From the shanties to the refuse and animals in the yards, Killian saw that the people along the tracks were obviously as poor as he was. He thought about the little over one hundred and fifty dollars he had been given and realized that he had more money than his whole family had ever had in a year. He vowed that when he got to Tennessee, he would write to his father and apologize for going against his wishes by coming to America. He remembered that he had promised his father that he would not use his earnings to get to America. Since he hadn't earned the money, he felt that he had not betrayed the promise. He also vowed to send him as much money as he possibly could.

As the train rolled into the countryside, it picked up speed. He was enjoying the view when he noticed a young mother sit down across the aisle with a toddler and a baby. The baby was crying and getting louder. The little boy started whining to go to the water closet, and the mother was trying to get the baby to stop crying, yet see to the needs of her son. Very flustered, she stood up, holding the baby, and took the boy by the hand.

Killian looked up at her. He said, "You seem to have your hands full. Can I help?"

No one else offered help. She looked as if she was confused about what she should do.

Killian looked down the aisle. He assured her, "There's no place I can go on a moving train. I'll be right here when you get back."

She smiled, and out of desperation, she handed him the baby. He held the baby, and she seemed to quiet down a bit. As he held her, he rubbed her stomach. He didn't know why, but he did. As he rubbed, he felt some heat, and the baby got quieter and quieter and finally stopped crying.

The woman came back a few minutes later and had a panicked look on her face. She had tried to find her seat in relation to the crying child, but since the baby wasn't crying, she almost walked past her seat. She stood there looking at the sleeping baby, amazed. She looked at Killian. She asked him, "How did you do that?"

Killian looked up. "I think she felt how stressed you were, and it frightened her." Killian assumed the baby was a little girl because of the pink blanket with ribbons on it.

The woman reached for the baby, but Killian held on to her. "Why don't you let her sleep, and you can get some rest and tend to the boy."

She smiled. "You're so kind. Do you have children?"

"No, I'm not married, but I have six brothers."

She raised her eyebrows. "Six? You must know a lot about babies. Are you the oldest?"

"No, ma'am, I'm actually the youngest, but some of my older brothers have children."

"Am I hearing an Irish accent?" she asked, smiling.

"Yes, ma'am. I only hesitate to tell you that because that usually starts a fight. You're not going to start a fight, are you?"

She laughed aloud. "No, I won't start a fight. I'm of German descent, but I live in a neighborhood where there are many Irish. They seem to be nice people, but a bit clannish. May I ask how old you are?"

Killian smiled. "I'm eighteen, but I'll be nineteen in eleven months and two weeks."

She laughed aloud again.

"Well, I'm only twenty, so please don't call me ma'am, OK?"

He smiled. "OK. What is your name?"

"Helen, Helen Hartman. I live with my husband and these two children in Knoxville, Tennessee."

"Knoxville? That's where I am going."

"And what takes you to Knoxville?"

"I'm going to try to find some or all of my uncles and see if I can get a job."

"How many uncles do you have?"

"Six, believe it or not." He laughed.

She looked at him. "Your grandmother had seven kids?"

"Yes, and me mother did too. I'm the youngest of the seven."

Helen looked up in thought. "Isn't there something about the seventh son of the seventh son? I've heard that somewhere before."

Killian shook his head. "I've not heard of it."

"Well, it doesn't matter. I want to give you my address. When we get to Knoxville, my husband will want to thank you for helping me, and if you don't find a job, maybe he can help you. He runs the stockyard there."

"Sure," Killian nodded with enthusiasm. As the train moved along, they got quiet, and Killian noticed that the little boy had fallen asleep. Helen was nodding off too. He looked down at the sleeping baby and smiled as he looked at her miniature features. Her eyes were closed, and the remnants of a smile were on her lips. She clutched one of Killian's fingers. Killian closed his eyes.

He was awakened when Helen took the baby. "Thank you so much. You've been a great help."

Killian nodded. "Don't hesitate to let me know if you need help, OK?"

She smiled and took the little boy's hand and started back toward the water closet. Killian dozed off again, and when he awoke, there were two women in the row where Helen had been sitting. He got up to go to the water closet and saw Helen sitting back about six rows. He stopped, and before he could say anything, she leaned toward him. "I went to change the baby, and when I got back, my seat had been taken."

Killian looked around to see if there were any empty seats around her, but there weren't. He looked back at her. "Still, let me know when I can help," he said.

She smiled and thanked him again. He went to the water closet and then returned to his seat.

About an hour later, he heard the baby crying again. He looked back, and Helen was trying to hush the baby. When she looked his way, he motioned to her to bring the baby. She smiled and shook her head. The baby continued to cry and got louder. He heard the crying get closer and turned to see Helen walking toward him. She handed him the baby, and when he put her on his shoulder, she quit crying immediately. He rubbed the baby's back and raised his eyes at Helen. She shook her head and went back to her seat with a grateful smile.

Killian felt the baby move her head and knew she wasn't asleep. He held the child where he could see her face, and she smiled real big. He had to smile back. Her eyes sparkled as she watched him, and she clutched one of his fingers again in her tiny fist. He rode along holding the baby's head, and the baby just looked around but didn't cry. After a while, Killian saw the baby's eyelids get heavy. He put her back on his shoulder, and she went back to sleep.

The woman across the aisle, who looked to be about Killian's age, had auburn hair in curls that lay down her back. Her starched white blouse made her look neat and proper. She looked at him with a smile. "You have a cute baby. How old is he, and what's his name?"

Killian looked at the baby. "It's a girl, and I have no idea how old she is or what her name is."

The woman frowned at him. "You have a baby and you don't know anything about it?"

Killian laughed. "It's not my baby. I'm not married. It belongs to the lady back a couple of rows. I'm just helping her out."

"Oh, I'm sorry. That's very nice of you."

The older woman, who had a sour look on her face and yellow teeth, leaned forward and said, "Jill, you shouldn't talk to strangers—especially men you don't know."

Jill looked forward. "Mother, I am twenty-one years old. I may talk to whomever I wish. Besides, any man who would help a lady out with a baby has got to be a nice person." She smiled at Killian.

The woman adjusted her bonnet. "It's not wise to converse with strangers is all I'm saying."

Killian moved over from the window seat to the aisle seat and extended his hand. "My name is Killian O'Rourke. I'm pleased to meet you."

Jill smiled. "My name is Jill Hasenyeager. How do you do?"

Killian smiled back and said, "Pleased to meet you."

Jill looked over at him. "I love the name Killian, and from your accent, I'm guessing you're from Ireland. Am I right?"

"I am from Ireland, as of a few days ago, and thank you."

"Is everybody in your family as redheaded as you are?"

He laughed. "Only my father. My brothers took after me…my mother."

"There's some folklore about the name Killian. I'm trying to remember what it is." Jill was looking at the ceiling of the train. She finally shook her head and said, "I can't remember."

Killian asked, "What is folklore?"

She smiled. "It's stories and tales about people and things from a particular region that many different people from different walks of life have heard, but the tales are generally unsupported by evidence or facts. Do you understand?"

Killian looked at her. "Not at all." But he smiled at her anyway.

She laughed aloud. "You're amusing."

She paused. "Well, if I heard that all seventh sons from Ireland are redheaded, and people from Tennessee, New York, and Texas said they had heard the same thing, then it would be folklore because no one has checked all the seventh sons of the seventh sons. Understand?"

Killian nodded his head in understanding. About that time, Helen came forward. "Let me have her. I don't want to be a burden on you."

Killian shook his head. "It's no burden; she just sleeps. Bring her back anytime."

Helen nodded with an appreciative smile and went back to her seat.

Killian wondered about this seventh son of the seventh son thing Jill was talking about. Mrs. O'Malley and Mrs. Brown had made note of it also.

Jill and her mother got off at the next stop, somewhere in the mountains that evening. The conductor wanted to know who wanted dinner, and he started sending people to the dining car as seats became available. Helen came back up and sat across from Killian now that the seat was empty. When the porter got to them, Killian stood up and said,

"Let me take the baby." He put her on his shoulder. She didn't let out a whimper.

"You have a way with babies. You shouldn't waste that talent."

"Oh yeah, I'll open up a nursery for mothers who have children that won't stop crying. That ought to make me rich and famous."

Helen laughed. "Well, I would certainly pay for your services." They were seated, and Killian ordered after Helen did. The sliced beef was a little tough, but the corn on the cob was dripping with butter and was delicious. He had green beans and sourdough bread. He watched Helen eat and felt that she was a refined lady. He watched his manners the best he knew how. The meal, overall, was pretty good, having been cooked aboard a train.

Helen finished and looked at him. "Excuse me," she said, and she took the baby and the little boy.

Killian looked at her. "Leave the bag; I'll bring it," he said.

She smiled, nodded, and walked off. He picked up the bag, got up, and went to the back of the dining car. "How much do I owe you for the dinner?" he asked the man at the cashbox.

The man looked at him a little surprised. "Your wife already paid for it."

Killian started to question the man, but realized that Helen had paid for his meal. He walked back to the car, and an elderly woman grabbed his wrist. "Did I hear someone say you were the seventh son of a seventh son?"

33

"Yes, ma'am, but—"

"Please. My Harold is having an awful time breathing."

Killian looked at the old man next to her; he was slumped over by the window with his eyes closed. He was in a rumpled suit that seemed to be too big for him. He was unshaven, and Killian could see the cigarette stains on his fingers. Killian was afraid he was dead.

"Ma'am, I'm not a doctor. I don't know what I can do."

She had fear in her eyes, and Killian could hear the man's ragged breathing. He reached over to see if he could feel the old man's heartbeat. He noticed that the man's chest was hot. He moved his hand around and never did find a heartbeat, but the old man coughed loudly and sat up. As he opened his eyes, his breathing wasn't labored anymore.

The old woman kissed his hand. "Oh, thank God for you. Thank you so much."

Killian looked at her in surprise. "But I didn't do anything."

The old woman looked back at him. "I understand. This will be our secret." She smiled and winked at him.

He walked away and sat down near Helen, thinking, "Poor woman. She has lost her mind. He started breathing better because he sat up."

Helen looked at him and asked, "Are you all right?"

"Yes, but why did you pay for my meal?" He was a little embarrassed that the woman had paid for his food.

She smiled. "For all you have done for me, it was the least I could do."

"Well, thank you, but don't do it anymore. I can pay for my meals."

She smiled again. "I'm sure you can."

The train ride took them through beautiful mountains. The train would stop long enough in small towns to load the mail and let passengers board or disembark. The forest was in full leaf, and there wild flowers of all colors in the open meadows. He helped Helen to the point that people thought that he was her husband. When they had to change trains, he would hold the baby, because she wouldn't cry with him holding her. Helen took care of the little boy, HJ.

Killian looked at the little boy. "What kind of a name is HJ?" he asked Helen

"It stands for Howard Junior. My husband's name is Howard.

Chapter 4

They were going through different states, and he learned that they were like counties in Ireland, but the states were divided up into sections called counties. They passed through Pennsylvania, Virginia, and North Carolina. They changed trains again, and Helen told him they would be in Tennessee in a matter of hours. Killian had never seen such mountains. There seemed to be fog in between the mountains, especially early in the mornings. Helen looked over and told him they were in Tennessee, and he noticed that it looked exactly like North Carolina and Virginia. After a few more hours, the train slowed, and the conductor announced, "Next stop, Knoxville, Tennessee, next stop."

The train pulled into a rustic-looking train station, where baggage handlers were waiting to try to make a little money and uniformed railroad personnel were busy writing on clipboards. Across from the station was a line of fine horses and carriages.

Killian got his suitcase down, picked up Helen's bag for her, and followed her off the train. A slim man ran up to her and hugged and kissed her. Killian was a little surprised because the man appeared to be about thirty-five years old. He was dressed better than most and wore a very stylish tan hat.

Helen turned to Killian. "Howard, I want you to meet Killian O'Rourke. He helped with the kids all the way from New York, and if he hadn't, I would have lost my mind. Little Grace was colicky, and she would only quit crying for him."

Howard shook his hand. "I appreciate all you've done for my family. How can I repay you?"

Killian shook his head. "'Twas no trouble at all. I was glad to help. I was wondering if you might know where the Irish community might be. I'm looking for my uncles."

Howard frowned in thought. "There are several areas in Knoxville where you couldn't swing a dead cat without hitting an Irishman."

Killian laughed.

"I could ask my foreman tomorrow," Howard said. "He's as Irish as they come. His name is John Meehan. Where are you staying?"

Killian shook his head again. "I don't have a place. Where is your stockyard, so that I can find you tomorrow?"

Howard motioned him over to the carriage. "There's a boardinghouse a few blocks from the stockyard. I will drop you there. You can walk down tomorrow, and we'll talk to John."

Killian expressed his appreciation and got into their fine carriage. He rode with them for about hour and a half. When it finally stopped, Killian got out with his suitcase and shook Howard's hand again. "I'll see you in the morning."

Helen shook his hand and held it. "I want to thank you from the bottom of my heart for all you have done for me. I don't think I could have done it without you. Good-bye and I hope to see you again someday."

Killian walked up to the door of the boardinghouse, breathing the smell of the stockyards, and a woman opened it after his knock. "Can I help you?"

Killian's heart jumped when he heard her Irish accent.

"Yes, ma'am, I was wondering if you had a room I might sleep in."

She smiled. "For an Irishman, I always have a room. Come in." She paused in the entryway. "I'm booked up, but you can share with Grandpa Walter. He's used to doubling up, so don't worry about him. Follow me." She added in a low voice, "We've already had supper, but come to the kitchen, and I'll find you a wee bit to eat."

He hoped it wasn't cabbage and potatoes. She took him to a room down a long, dark hallway, and there was a big bed with an old man sleeping on the far side of it. The house was showing its age, but it was very clean. She pointed and said, "Drop your kit there and come with me."

He followed her to the kitchen. She was a heavyset woman with gray hair pulled up into a bun. She had little spectacles on her nose, and her dress and apron went all the way to the floor. She looked at him as she prepared the food. "From your accent, I'd say you recently arrived from the old country, have you not?"

"Yes, ma'am. I spent one night in New York and then got on a train for Tennessee. I'm sorry I didn't introduce myself, but I'm Killian." He decided to leave out his middle initial from then on and finished with, "O'Rourke."

"Well, you can call me Mary. O'Shaunnessy is the last name. What brings you to Knoxville?"

"I'm here to find any of my uncles and try to find a job, hopefully."

"And how many uncles would you be having?"

"Six of them and their families."

Mary smiled again. "Six? Oh my, that is a lot. O'Rourke? I know the name from somewhere, but I can't recall," she said, looking up at the ceiling. "Well, no mind. I'll think of it later."

Killian looked at her. "Do you know the story behind the seventh son of the seventh son?"

Her eyes widened. "Some say he is a charmer who can attract anyone to liking him. He can also be a healer or may know of the future to come. He might even possess all the powers. Why do you ask?"

Killian was hesitant to tell her. "I never heard of it in Ireland. It wasn't until I got here that I heard the stories, and I was wondering about it."

"Well, if you ever come across a seventh son of a seventh son, hold on to him. He has powers you've never seen, and he's certain to be Irish."

Killian understood why the old woman on the train acted as she did when she thought he had healed her husband.

He went to bed with Grandpa Walter and slept soundly. He awoke the next morning, changed clothes, and went down to breakfast. He wasn't used to eggs and bacon and biscuits. What he thought was a roll, they called a biscuit. What he called a biscuit, they called a cracker.

Mary asked him how long he would stay. "I don't know. Until my money runs out or I find a relative. I'm going to the stockyard to talk to a man who might know something. Can I leave my case in the room?"

"Certainly you may, and good luck today."

Killian walked down the street toward the stockyards, which he could still smell that morning. It was farther than he thought, and it took him about forty-five minutes to get there. At the stockyards, he saw pen after pen filled with cattle. There were some goats in one pen and horses in another. He saw Howard watching some cattle being unloaded, and he walked up and waited for him to finish.

When Howard saw Killian, he turned and shouted, "John, come over here please!" A big man with a beard and a cigar walked over, and Howard looked at Killian. "This young man is just in from Ireland and is looking for family. Can you help him?"

John took the cigar out of his mouth. "Depends on who he's looking for and if I know them. What's the name, son?"

Killian looked over at him. "O'Rourke. There's six brothers, and they all have families."

"Oh, there's an O'Rourke clan out toward the mountain that has a passel of brothers. Old man Thomas is the head of the clan. They don't like anyone who's not family to enter into their kingdom." He laughed. "It's part of Knoxville, but you have go to outside the city to get there."

Killian's heart skipped a beat. He knew that his grandfather was named Thomas, even though he had never met him. "Where can I find this mountain?"

John pointed. "You see that road over there? Well, don't take it; it'll do you no good. Take that road there out about eight miles, and you will come to a turnoff that says Mountain Road Cutoff. Take that out about four miles, and you will come to a little settlement of about 300 people, and the O'Rourke clan will be on the first road on the left. That's shorter than going through the city."

Killian nodded. "I'll start walking tomorrow morning. I should be there in four or five hours."

John looked down at him from atop the pen. "That's a lot of walking. What are you going to do if it's not them?"

"Walk back, I suppose." Killian went back to the boardinghouse in time for supper. He sat at a big table with two women and eight other men. Mary told him after supper that she had moved his bag downstairs, and he could have a room by himself that night. He was glad of that. He thought about the fact that he had slept with brothers all his life.

Chapter 5

The next morning, he told Mary what he was going to do and he paid her the dollar for the two nights. As he left, she gave him a cloth sack with a couple of sandwiches in it. He thanked her and walked down to the stockyards. He didn't see Howard, so he kept walking. Three hours later, he came to the Mountain Road Cutoff. The road was uphill, as was the road he had to take. Both had seen heavy traffic, according to the wheel ruts. The road ran along a meadow of wildflowers that gave off a sweet aroma. He saw deer standing at the tree line up the hill and two raccoons romping together. He was amazed at the beauty of the country and the abundance of wildlife.

He turned right and started again. It was an uphill climb as far as he could see. He wished he had a rucksack to carry his clothes in. A suitcase was cumbersome and bulky, but he kept going, switching hands often. He passed a mountain stream, so he sat down on a log, ate the two sandwiches Mary had made for him, and he knelt down and drank the water. It was cold and tasted better than any water he'd ever had before.

He came to his first left an hour and a half later. He turned and walked down the road. He saw houses on both sides of the road, and they were all pretty similar. At the end of the road, there was a big house facing him. On the porch sat an old man in a rocker. He held a cane in his hand. As Killian walked toward the house, he saw the old man give a shrill whistle and point at him. About that time, three men came out of houses on the left and three came out of the houses on the right. They lined up in front of him. When he got to them, one of them asked, "Who are you, and where do you think you're going?"

Killian looked at them and didn't show fear. He figured that he would get beaten in a fight with six men, but he would make an impression nonetheless. "I'm looking for Thomas O'Rourke. Am I going to have to kick the shit out of all six of you to get by?"

The one that was doing the talking smiled. "I hope not. What do you want with him?"

"He's my grandfather, and I have a message from my papa. Now, do you want to go up and tell him, or should I go through you and tell him myself?"

The man smiled again. "Wait here," he said. He started to walk away, but stopped and turned. "What's your name?"

"I'll tell him that when I get there." The man smiled again and started toward the old man. Killian saw him talk to the old man and point his way. Then the man rose up and signaled him to come forward. Killian looked at the men in front of him. "Excuse me," he said, and walked through the line of men, bumping shoulders with two of them.

He walked toward the house, and the old man looked at him. "What is your name, boy?"

"Killian G. O'Rourke, sir."

The old man paused a minute. "What's your father's name?"

"Barron O'Rourke, sir."

The old man thought a minute and said to the other man, "Leave us." He looked Killian over. "Come up here and put your case down and sit."

Killian walked up, dropped his suitcase with a thud, and sat in the rocker next to the old man. Killian looked over at him. "Are you Thomas O'Rourke?"

"I am."

"Are ye my grandfather?"

"I am."

Killian sat there quietly, trying to let his grandfather have the next word. The old man wore a rumpled coat to match his pants. A wide leather belt held up his pants, and his boots looked in need of polish. The old man hadn't shaved in a couple of days, and the hair on his head was gray with barely a tint of brown.

Thomas looked straight ahead. "What do you want here?"

"To find you and try and get a job so I can send money back home."

Thomas looked at him. "With six uncles, you should be able to get a job, but there's no guarantee that out of six brothers, any of them will cooperate."

Killian turned his head. "Oh, don't I know it."

The old man seemed irritated. "What would you know about dealing with six brothers? I haven't heard from Barron in many years, but at last count, he had four sons. I haven't heard your name before, so I'm assuming you're number five. Correct?"

Killian waited a moment before he answered. "No, sir. Garr is number five."

"Then you're number six? How's your mother?"

Killian kept his voice calm. "She died last year, and Geoffrey is number six."

The old man stood up with the help of his cane and stepped over to face Killian. Killian saw that he was a tall man, even at his age. "You mean to tell me you're the seventh son?"

"Of the seventh son. Yes, sir."

Thomas looked around to see if anyone was within earshot. "Never tell anybody that. Do you hear me? Never."

Killian nodded. "OK for now, but someone is going to have to tell me someday why that is so important."

The grandfather leaned toward him. "I'm trying to keep you alive. You go telling that around and you won't last long, that I can guarantee."

"Why would anyone want to harm me for my birth order?"

"It's something I'll have to explain in time."

Killian shifted in the rocking chair. "Now would be as good as any time I can think of."

Thomas sat back down and was silent for a few minutes. "Did you tell anyone else about this? Anyone else at all?"

"The two women who paid for my train fare asked me about the six uncles I was looking for, and then one of them asked me who I left behind, and I told them about my six brothers. I guess they can count. Another lady on the train asked me about it, but she said it was folklore. An older woman heard us talking about it and asked me to look at her

46

husband. He was breathing something awful. I told her I was no doctor and I couldn't do anything, but she insisted. I checked to see if I could find his heartbeat, and as I was feeling his chest, he woke up and then sat up and started breathing normally. She thought I did it."

Thomas looked at him. "Didn't ya?"

"No, sir. It was just the fact that he sat up; then he could breathe better."

Thomas looked off down the road. "Did you touch anyone or do anything else on the train?"

"Yes, sir. A lady had a baby she couldn't get to stop crying. I held the baby, and she quit crying. She brought her to me several times. They live here in Knoxville, and she said her husband might give me a job at his stockyard, but I would have to find a horse to get there."

Thomas shook his head. "No. You'll not be working."

Before Killian could say anything else, he saw the six uncles walking toward him.

They stopped, and one said, "Well, is this the long-lost relative from Ireland now?"

Thomas nodded. "Yes, he's the fifth child of my youngest son, Barron."

"Well, boy," the man said again, "where do you think you're going to live? We have no room for you and no job for you."

Thomas looked at them. "He'll be staying with me, and he won't need a job. I'll take care of all his needs."

All six uncles frowned. One asked, "Why?"

"Because I said so, I don't have to explain myself to the likes of you. Now go home and deal with those whiny kids you have."

The uncles still had frowns on their faces, but they turned and walked off.

Killian looked at his grandfather again. "I need a job. I need to send money home to Pa."

"Why does he need money? Doesn't he have the farm?"

"Yes, but it doesn't produce enough to feed a family our size. I'm the only one who hasn't married, so they all have wives, and some have kids. I had a job digging potatoes twelve hours a day for ten shillings. It cost more than that to feed me, so he let me go to the coast to find a job."

Thomas rubbed his whiskers. "I'm surprised he let you come to America."

Killian shook his head. "He didn't. I promised I wouldn't get a job and use the money to pay for the fare to America."

"But you did anyway, huh?"

"No, sir. I pulled a young boy from in front of galloping horses, and his grandfather bought me new clothes, paid my fare, and gave me ten dollars to get here."

"So you saved a child, helped a woman with a crying baby, and saved an old man from dying on the train."

Killian shook his head. "I happened to be there when all of that happened. I didn't do anything special."

"So your gifts have not been revealed to you yet?"

Killian frowned and said, "What gifts are you talking about?"

Thomas looked at him. "You're the seventh son of the seventh son. You're ordained by God with special gifts. Sometimes it is one gift, and sometimes you can have two or more. From what you told me, you have the gift of healing, for sure. You may develop the gift of seeing the future. I don't know, but you must be on the watch for these gifts. You have to realize that you're special. Your father knew that. That's why he didn't want you coming to America."

Killian thought about what his grandfather had just said. "I don't believe in this. All the things that happened can easily be explained. I don't have any gifts. This is why my father told me that if I went to America, I would be made a clown or look like a freak. Is that what you're going to do?"

Thomas frowned. "If people find out who you are, they will be bringing every little ache and pain to you, and if they even think that you helped them, they are going to tell everyone they know; and then those people will tell everyone *they* know, and there will be no stopping it. Others will think you're a devil if you don't praise God as the source of your gifts. Listen to me very carefully. Do not talk of being the seventh son of a seventh son to anyone. Do you hear?"

Killian nodded his head.

"Do you understand why?"

Again, Killian nodded his head. He let all that soak in. "I need to do my part and help my family. I need a job."

Thomas looked straight ahead. "If you got a job, you couldn't send more than thirty dollars a month to them."

"That's a dollar a day. That will help them tremendously."

"I don't want you working because you will be exposed. You may see the people you met on the train. I'll give you thirty dollars a month to send home. Come in the house, and let me get you situated with a place to sleep. You can write home, and I'll give you some money. Come on."

Thomas opened the door to a room. There was a bed in the middle, a dresser, and a basin and towel. The curtains were drawn across the window, and there was a small closet for his clothes. It smelled as if it had been closed up for a time, so Killian opened the window to let fresh air in. "My room is right next door, if you need me. When you get settled in, come to the kitchen. Gretchen will fix you something to eat."

Killian looked around. "Who's Gretchen?"

"My wife, but she is not your grandmother. Your grandmother died seven years ago." Thomas paused. "You think it's a coincidence that you showed up seven years after her death?"

Killian looked at him. "Yes, sir, I do. It's just a coincidence."

Over the next few days, Killian and Thomas walked the grounds and talked of his father growing up in Ireland. Killian was surprised to learn that his grandfather decided to move his whole family to America, but his father refused to go because of his mother's desire to stay.

As they walked, Killian realized that his grandfather must be rich, at least by Ireland's standards. The house and grounds were almost as big as his father's farm. The uncles lived on smaller but just as impressive estates.

Killian had gotten paper and pen from his grandfather, and he sat down to compose a letter to his father.

Dear Papa,

I'm in America. I want to ask your forgiveness because I know you didn't want me here. I didn't earn the money and spend it on the fare. A man purchased a ticket and gave it to me for saving his grandson's life from a runaway carriage. I took that as I sign that I should go to America. I got to New York and found that many people don't like the Irish. I was taken in by an Irish woman, who pitied my plight. Her friends donated money for my train ticket to Knoxville, Tennessee, where some kind folks helped me locate my uncles and my grandfather. You never told me my grandfather was still alive. I got a poor reception from my uncles, but my grandfather took me in and has given me a place to live. There's one hundred and fifty dollars enclosed. I hope this will help what I was not able to do before. I will send more, but it will be in smaller amounts of thirty dollars. One hundred and twenty dollars is from the donations to get me to Tennessee, and thirty dollars is from Grandpa Thomas. He said he would give me the money to send to you because he doesn't want me working.

Again, I ask your forgiveness, but things are so much better here than there.

Love,

Killian

Killian sealed the letter and put it in his pocket to put in the post himself. He didn't trust anyone else to do it. He went to bed that night and dreamed that he was walking in the woods. He saw something lying under a railroad trestle. When he got a closer look, he saw that it was a young girl. She was dead, and someone had covered her up with her red coat. All of a sudden, he woke up. The dream seemed so real. He lay there wide-awake, and the next thing he knew, Thomas was shaking him. "'Tis seven o'clock. What time do you normally get up?"

Killian looked up. "Sorry, Grandpa. I usually get up to be at work by five. I don't know what happened."

"Well, you don't have to be anywhere by five or even seven, but you miss the best part of the day sleeping until seven."

Killian got up and got dressed and decided not to say anything about the dream to Thomas. He went in the kitchen for breakfast, and Gretchen had cooked eggs and bacon and potatoes, but these potatoes were fried and not boiled. He was glad that he wasn't eating porridge anymore.

They sat on the porch and when Thomas's oldest son, Patrick, stopped by, Thomas looked over at Killian. "Paddy, take some money and go to the stockyard and buy the boy a horse." Patrick was a bigger man than his father was. He was handsome. His coal-black hair was combed back and trimmed above his collar. Unlike most men, he was clean-shaven.

Paddy looked at him rather strangely.

Thomas nodded his head and told him, "Get him a tall horse. He's not through growing yet."

Patrick walked back to his house next door, saddled his horse, and rode out. Patrick seemed to be a lot like Thomas. He didn't seem to have the animosity toward Killian that his brothers had. He didn't look at Killian with suspicion as they all did, and he seemed to sense that Thomas had a good reason for doing what he was doing.

Killian was over six feet two inches tall, and none of his uncles was more than five feet eight; some were shorter. Killian looked his grandfather in the eye. "Thanks, Grandpa, but I wish I could work and save the money to pay for things like that."

Thomas leaned back in his rocker. "You would have to have a horse to get a job anyway, so don't fret over it."

That afternoon, Patrick came back leading a big red horse. The horse was tall, and his long legs made him look fast. Thomas looked at the horse with Killian and Patrick. "This is a good choice. A fine horse," he said.

Patrick looked at his father. "When I signed the bill of sale, the man at the stockyards asked me if I knew of a Killian O'Rourke."

Thomas looked concerned. "What did you tell him?"

Patrick looked at both of them. "I told him I never heard of him."

"That's good. Ye done well, Paddy. Thanks."

The next day, Killian and Thomas were sitting on the porch, and Patrick came home from work and rode up to Thomas's house. "A girl from across the road and down a ways was abducted. She went to school and hasn't been seen since yesterday. They are forming a search party to look for her. The sheriff wants some to go east and some go west and search.

Thomas nodded. "Bring our horses up and send five of your brothers east and you ride with me and the boy west."

Patrick nodded, went back to his house, and returned leading the two horses. Killian's horse did not have a saddle, but Patrick had made a bridle out of rope.

Thomas looked at Killian. "You'll have to ride bareback until I can get you a saddle."

Killian smiled and led the horse to the side of the porch where he could climb on him. The horse's back came almost up to Killian's chin.

Thomas saw him smile. "What's so amusing?"

"I've never ridden a horse with a saddle before."

"You're saying your family was so poor they couldn't afford a saddle?"

Killian adjusted the bridle on the horse's neck. "No, sir. I'm saying we were so poor we couldn't afford a horse."

Thomas shook his head and mounted his horse. Patrick stopped and told his brothers to go east and meet back at sundown. They rode off into the fields of tall grass and trees. Killian rode silently, but he wondered what the uncles thought of him. He knew that what Thomas was doing for him was way out of the ordinary. They searched hills and hollows and up and down mountainsides until it started to get dark.

Thomas looked up at the failing light. "Well, let's go back. I want to get back before dark," he said. They rode up to the house about thirty minutes before sundown. As they got off the horses, the second-oldest brother, Dean, came riding up at a gallop.

He stopped in front of them. "They found her about an hour ago. She's dead. The sheriff said it appeared she had been violated and murdered. The sheriff was asking about anyone new to the area, and he was mentioned." He pointed at Killian. "They'll be coming to talk with him soon."

Thomas looked at Dean. "Where did they find her?"

"They spotted her under a railroad trestle by her red coat."

Killian's ears started to burn, and he thought that he was going to throw up. He dropped his horse's rope and started walking toward the house so they wouldn't see him cry.

"Give your reins to your uncle and—" He looked around, and Killian was walking up the porch steps. "Paddy, take the horses and put them up. The rest of you go on home."

Thomas walked up to the house as fast as he could walk with his cane. He went in and grabbed Killian, turned him around to face him, and saw tears running down his face. "What's wrong, boy?"

Killian could hardly talk. He stuttered through his sobs. "Two nights ago I had a dream. I was walking in the woods, and I came upon a dead girl with a red coat over her under a railroad trestle. It was her. I should have said something. I could have saved her." He started crying uncontrollably.

Thomas shook him by his shoulders. "Listen to me and listen good. Can you stop crying long enough to listen?"

Killian nodded.

"If you had come in here claiming to be the seventh son of a seventh son, they would hang you for this murder. If they find out you had a dream about it two nights ago, they'll still hang you. Do you see what I'm saying about trying to save your life?"

Killian nodded, knowing that Grandpa Thomas was an ally and not an enemy.

Thomas went to shut the door. "Oh shit. The sheriff is coming. Dry your eyes and stay in here unless I call you out. Do you understand?"

Killian nodded and sat down. Thomas walked out and sat down in his chair on the porch.

The sheriff and a young deputy came riding up. "Thomas, we want to speak to your grandson." The sheriff was an unshaved man whose belly hung over his belt slightly. The deputy looked as if he had on new everything, from his white Stetson down to his shiny new boots.

"About what?" Thomas replied.

"I'll tell you when I see him. Now where is he?"

Thomas sat there a few seconds. "Killian, come out here, please," he called.

Killian walked outside.

The sheriff looked at him. "Why are your eyes so red, boy? You been crying?"

Thomas looked at the sheriff. "He's been in bed for three days with a cold. Two nights ago, I sat up with him all night long."

The sheriff cut his eyes toward Thomas and then back at Killian. "Two nights ago, you say?"

Thomas nodded.

"The doc said she was killed two days ago. Anyone else see him in his sickbed?"

"My six sons. Do you want me to bring them out?"

The sheriff shook his head. "No, if it wasn't true, the lot of you wouldn't tell me."

"Sheriff, you have a killer to catch. Hadn't you need to be about your duly elected business?"

The sheriff said nothing but turned his horse and rode out with the deputy.

Thomas watched them ride down the road. "Killian, if you have any more visions, tell me about them and don't wait until morning. Wake me up and let me know. Do you hear?"

Killian nodded.

Killian rode with Thomas into town the next day. People stared at him. The word had spread that there was a death in the community, and only one new person had arrived of late.

Two weeks later, Killian had a vision that he saw a man running after a woman by a railroad track. He knew it was in town because he could see the buildings. The man caught her and hit her on the head with a club. He turned her over and started taking her clothes off, but then he stopped. A train was coming. So he dragged her around behind a metal railroad-equipment box. The train roared through, and suddenly Killian woke up. He didn't want to get out of bed, but he was afraid not to.

He shook his grandfather, who woke with a start.

Killian had tears in his eyes. "Grandpa, I had another vision."

Thomas got up and lit a lamp. "Tell me about it, and don't leave out any details."

Killian spoke slowly with his eyes closed, visualizing each step of the dream.

Thomas looked at the floor. "A train at night? Was it going fast or slow? And was it midnight-dark or what?"

"The train was going fast, and I could see down the track a ways, so it wasn't totally dark."

Thomas nodded. "The only train that goes straight through is the southbound train, and it goes through at dusk on Thursdays, so the murder hasn't been done yet. The only thing to do is get you out of town on Thursday."

Killian looked at his grandfather. "Can't you tell someone and see if we can prevent it?"

"No, no, no. It doesn't work that way. You cannot change the future; you can only see it. Let me think on this some. Don't say anything to anyone; you understand?"

Killian nodded and went back to bed, but he wasn't sleepy. He lay in bed wondering about the dreams. Thomas called them visions. Could it be real that he could see the future? It scared him.

The next day was Wednesday, so Thomas and Killian rode into town. "Tell me if you see the place where the murder takes place."

As they rode toward the tracks, Killian saw the woman in his dreams walk out of the store. He tugged on Thomas's sleeve and pointed her out with a nod.

"Don't look at her," Thomas said. "Just keep riding."

Killian seemed to be in pain. "Are you sure there isn't something we can do to—"

"No. I told you why."

They came to the train tracks, and Killian pointed, saying, "That's it right there. See the box to the left? That's where he drug her after he hit her."

Thomas looked back down the tracks. "Which way was the train going?"

Killian pointed.

"That's south, and that will be the way the train will be headed," Thomas said. "Did you see the man's face? How tall was he?"

Killian shook his head. "No, I only saw her face as she looked back at the man chasing her. She was screaming for help. He had on blue jeans, a white shirt, and a dark hat."

Thomas frowned. "That describes half the men in Knox County. Let's go back to the house."

They turned and rode back to the house, and neither one talked. When they got back, they left the horses tied up out front and sat on the porch.

Thomas frowned. "Tomorrow is Thursday. We'll leave town at one and ride over to a saddlemaker near Strawberry Plain. It will take us until four o'clock to get there. We'll dicker over the price of the saddle for close to an hour, and at five o'clock, you tell me you're hungry. We'll go over to the diner across the street and spend an hour there. Then it will be too late to come back, so we'll find a place to stay and ride out at eight Friday morning so everyone there can see us. If your dream happens, and it will, they'll have to suspect someone else besides you."

Killian loved sitting on the porch and talking to his grandfather. Thomas told about his leaving Ireland and getting the ironworks started and then the gristmill and the market. Killian realized that his grandfather was a very smart man. They finally went to bed.

Thomas told his son Patrick what they were going to do about the saddle. The next day, Thomas told Killian to go over to Patrick's barn and get the horses. Killian brought them back, and they mounted up and started out. Thomas waved to several people and spoke to them as they went through town. When one man asked where he was off to, Thomas replied

in a loud voice, "We're on the way to the saddlemaker in Strawberry Plain.
"

They took the road to Strawberry Plain and arrived at the precise time Thomas said they would. Thomas dickered with Alvin, the saddlemaker, over a plain and simple saddle. At five, Killian looked at Thomas and said, "I'm getting hungry, Grandpa."

Thomas offered his final price for the saddle and told Alvin that he would throw in supper at the diner. They agreed on the deal and started toward the diner. They finished eating about six.

Thomas looked up in the sky. "It's too late to head back. Is there a boardinghouse near?"

Alvin, who was a short, rotund man in overalls with a tobacco juice-stained beard, frowned. "I insist you come to my house. I have plenty of room, and my missus won't mind at all."

The next morning, they got up at six, and Killian saddled both horses, admiring his new saddle and bridle. He mounted his horse and led Thomas's horse out to him. Thomas stood and talked with Alvin until the town started moving at about eight. He bade Alvin farewell and rode out so everyone could see him.

They got back to Knoxville about eleven and rode to the house. People were still staring. They tied the horses up and heard horses galloping down the street. It was the sheriff and his deputy. The sheriff reined his horse in.

"I want to talk to your grandson again. Where were you last night about dusk?"

Thomas leaned on his cane. "He was with me over in Strawberry Plain buying this saddle. Why do you want to know?"

The sheriff narrowed his eyes. "What time did you get there, and more importantly, what time did you leave?" The sheriff and deputy dismounted.

Thomas rubbed his whiskers. "We got there at four, bought the saddle about five, went to eat with Alvin, and then spent the night with him. We left about eight this morning and just now arrived back. Why do you want to know?"

The sheriff looked at Killian. "Madeline Harper was murdered last night." He paused. "In much the same way the other girl was."

"Wouldn't it be better to find the person who did it rather than a person you can pin it on?"

The sheriff turned red in the face, but just stared at Killian.

Killian looked him in the eye. "Excuse me. I'll put the horses up."

The sheriff barked at him, "Just stand where you are until I get through with you."

Killian picked up his and Thomas's reins and started toward the barn. The deputy grabbed his shoulder. "The sheriff said to—"

He didn't finish his sentence because Killian slugged him in the nose. The deputy went down, hit flat on his back, and didn't move.

The sheriff's mouth was open. "I'll arrest you for striking an officer of the law."

Killian looked the sheriff in the eye. He somehow knew that the sheriff would back down. He could feel it in his inner being. "No you won't," he said. Killian felt a boldness, but didn't know why he faced the sheriff down. It was as if a power had come over him. He turned and led the horses off toward Patrick's barn.

The sheriff looked at Thomas as if he were asking for help, and he didn't know why he didn't arrest Killian.

Thomas looked at the sheriff. "Two things, Sheriff: One, you need to teach this deputy not grab people without just cause, or he will get knocked on his ass every time. Second, you need to do your job and look for the killer. I know that's hard, but you can't pin every crime on somebody because they are new to the area. Feel lucky it wasn't you that grabbed him."

"Why is that?"

"Because you'd be lying there instead of him. Oh, there is something else you need to remember, and that is you are up for reelection this fall, aren't you? What's going to happen when the people realize you're not doing your job? You've already lost the votes on this road. Be careful how many people you wrongly accuse."

The sheriff bent over, slapped the deputy on the face, and brought him to. He helped him onto his horse and led him out.

Killian came back, and Thomas smiled. "What made you hit that deputy?"

"I didn't like him grabbing me."

"How did you know you wouldn't be arrested?"

Killian thought for a moment. "I didn't. I had a feeling come over me that I was right and I needed to stand my ground. I don't understand why I did that." He went into the house. Thomas smiled and followed him in.

The next morning, as Thomas and Killian sat on the porch, Thomas said, "I need to bring Paddy in on this. If something happens to me, I want somebody to look after you. Besides, he has a good head on him."

When they saw Patrick riding home from work, Thomas raised his cane in the air, and Patrick rode over to them. He seemed to be favoring his left shoulder.

"Come up on the porch and sit down," Thomas told his son. "I have something to talk to you about."

Patrick got off his horse, went up on the porch, and sat on the other side of Thomas.

"I've gotten something that's too big for me to think about by myself." Thomas looked down for a few minutes and then continued, "Killian here is the seventh son of Barron's. Do you know what that means?"

Patrick started to speak, but Thomas interrupted him. "Yes. That's it exactly. Have you ever wondered if it was true?"

Patrick shook his head. "No, I never considered it to be true. Still don't."

"He dreamed about that girl in the red coat being killed two nights before it happened. He dreamed about that Harper girl dying two nights before it happened. I figured out when that was going to happen and got him out of town until the next day. Can you explain that? I mean, he woke me up and described it in detail."

Patrick sat there rubbing his left shoulder.

Thomas looked at his arm. "Hurt your shoulder again?"

Patrick just nodded.

Killian stood up. "Come inside and take your shirt off."

Patrick looked at Killian as if he was crazy, but Thomas told Patrick, "Do it." They both got up and walked into the house.

Patrick took his shirt off and sat down.

Killian placed both hands on Patrick's shoulder. It felt hot, as the baby's stomach and the old man's chest had. He rubbed gently until the heat went away. He stepped back. "How does that feel now?"

Patrick stood up, moving his shoulder back and forth and then up and down. He looked at Killian. "How did you do that? What did you do to me?"

Thomas stepped up. "It has been revealed that so far that he has at least two gifts. One is to be able to see into the future, and the other is the power of healing. You understand that if this gets out, they will accuse him of heresy, and if they don't hang him, there will be a line of people from here to Ireland wanting to be cured." Thomas stood there for a few minutes. "But if you tell anyone, it may be his death. Think about it and let me know in the morning if you will help us."

Patrick put his shirt on, walked out, got on his horse, and rode toward his barn, still moving his shoulder to see if it was going to hurt.

Killian watched Patrick ride off. "Do you think he will tell anyone?"

"No. That bad shoulder has been a thorn in his side for many years. That will convince him. You were right to do that, but let me know before you do it again."

Killian nodded.

Killian knew that he had the powers now, and that they weren't something that just happened. This seemed to give him a new sense of self-awareness. Still, he wondered about it.

The next morning, Patrick came over before he left for work. When he stopped, Thomas asked, "How's the shoulder?"

Patrick smiled. "It's been so long since it felt good, I forgot how good felt." He looked down at his boots. "OK. I'll help you. What do you want me to do?"

"Nothing for the time being, but we will need to figure out a strategy if something else comes up. See if you can calm your brothers down and get them off his back."

Patrick narrowed his eyes. "They all came over last night and asked me if I would talk to you about Killian. They want to know why you have taken him in and don't make him work. We've never been treated that way and have never seen you treat anyone—especially your other grandsons—that way. Do you see why they're worried about you?"

Thomas nodded. "Well, that's how you will help. Figure out how to get off his back without telling them why. How you're going to do that, I don't know."

Patrick left, and Thomas told Killian to get the horses.

Killian walked over to the barn, and as he was saddling the horses, Uncle Dean walked in.

"Who said you could put your horse in this barn?" Dean asked.

Killian just looked over at him and said nothing.

Dean was irritated. "Don't ignore me. I'll knock your teeth out."

As he limped around the horse, Killian saw that he was limping with his left leg. Killian grabbed the reins and started backing the horse out. Dean got red in the face and drew back his fist, but before he could throw it at his nephew, Killian kicked him in the left knee. Dean yelled and fell to the floor. He lay there holding his knee, screaming in pain.

Killian backed his horse out, picked up the reins of his grandfather's horse, and walked the animals back to the house.

Thomas came out of the house and strode quickly toward the barn. "I thought I heard someone screaming."

"You did. It's Uncle Dean. He's lying over in Patrick's stable, holding his injured knee."

Thomas looked toward the stable. "What happened to him?"

Killian looked his grandfather in the eye. "He said he was going to knock my teeth out, so when he came up to do it, I kicked him in the knee."

67

Thomas shook his head. "That dumb bastard. I don't know what I'm going to do with him."

About that time, Dean's wife came out and looked around because she'd heard the screaming too. Thomas pointed to the barn, and she ran over there.

Thomas mounted. "Let's get out of here before you have to kick her in the knee also. She has an Irish temper."

They rode down the street and turned left. Killian had never been that way before. After a short ride, they turned onto a road that went downhill. At the bottom, a factory sat beside a river. A big sign read: O'Rourke's Iron Works. "One of the family businesses," Thomas said.

"One of them? How many do you have?"

Thomas looked down the river. "That grist mill down there is ours also. We own a market in town that sells vegetables and such, and I'm thinking of opening a dry goods store, if Marvin Crater doesn't straighten up and treat people right. Those three things keep all the men employed, plus what women in the family who want to work."

They rode back toward town and went to the dry goods store. They went in, and Thomas pointed, saying, "Pick out some jeans or work pants, some shirts, and boots. You'll need a broad-brimmed hat to keep the sun off of you."

After they had made their purchases, Killian tied them on the back of his horse and put on his new Stetson. Killian was amazed at the high prices of things. Eight dollars for a Stetson and one dollar for six pairs of white socks.

They rode into downtown Knoxville. When they got to the stockyards, Killian heard someone call his name. He saw it was Howard, and Helen was with him. On the way over, Killian told Thomas that she was the woman on the train with the baby. The baby was crying when they got there and climbed off their horses.

Helen looked at her husband. "Howard, I want to show you something."

She handed the baby to Killian. When Killian put the baby on his shoulder, she quit crying.

"See? I told you. He has a natural way with babies."

Killian handed the baby back to her mother and introduced Thomas to the couple. Howard asked if Killian was still looking for a job.

"No, sir, I'll be working at my family's mill."

Howard looked deep in thought. "Oh, you're one of those O'Rourkes. I'm sorry. I didn't realize that. There are a lot of O'Rourkes in this town, you got to admit."

Thomas and Killian just nodded. They bid the Hartmans a good day and rode back toward the house. On the way back, Thomas looked over at Killian. "Avoid those people if you can," he said.

Killian just nodded. He realized that everything he had done to heal people was because his gifts were emerging from whatever higher power had chosen him to bear them. That gave him a sense of power but also scared him.

Chapter 6

It was seven days later that Killian had another vision. He saw himself going down the main road in town, and he saw a woman go in the side door of a building. He woke up wondering what the significance was. There was no danger; no one died, and vision seemed just a few seconds long. He didn't wake Thomas as he'd been told to, but he told him about it the next morning.

Thomas thought on it for a while and shook his head. "I don't know what to think of it either. We'll just have to wait and see."

Two days later, Thomas and Killian rode their horses into town and went to the market that the family owned. Thomas saw his son and daughter-in-law who ran it and said to Killian, "Ride down to the post office and check for mail. I won't be but a minute here."

Killian rode down the main street to the post office. There was a letter from his father. He put it in his pocket and started back. He had gone about five hundred feet when he saw people running down a side street. Then he saw smoke coming out of an old, dilapidated building. He rode closer to see what was happening, and that's when he saw a door on the side of the building. It was the door in his vision. He thought, "Is there a woman in there?"

He couldn't take a chance that a woman was inside and might be overcome by smoke. He jumped off his horse, tied it to a rail, and ran across the street to the door. It was locked, so he backed up and kicked it in. The doorframe shattered, and the door flew off its hinges. Smoke poured out, but he ran in anyway.

People were yelling at him, telling him that it was an abandoned building.

"No one is in there!" one man yelled.

Killian walked down the hall. He had to stoop down—and finally to crawl—to get out of the smoke. He didn't see anything and had started back when he saw the woman lying at the bottom of the stairs. He grabbed her under her arms and started crawling backward, pulling her along. When he pulled her out the door, people ran over to help him. He collapsed from breathing in smoke, and someone helped him up and walked him across the street. He looked at the man who had helped him, and it was Thomas.

"Why did you go in there?" Thomas looked back at the door and realized it was the vision Killian had had. Orange flames were coming out of all windows and doors. They had to move back farther because of the heat. Thomas looked around. "Where's your horse?" he asked.

Killian looked at the rail where he had tied the horse, but he wasn't there. Then a man came walking up, leading Killian's horse.

"Is this your horse? I had to move him back because of the heat."

Thomas thanked him because Killian was still coughing from the smoke. Thomas put his hand under Killian's arm. "Let's get you out of here."

As they walked back to where Thomas had left his horse, people were patting Killian on the back. Thomas helped Killian up on his horse and took the reins as he mounted his own horse. He led Killian back to the house. As they rode back, Thomas shook his head. "I don't know what to say. I know you had to save that woman, but we have to keep people from noticing you for any reason, whether it be a as murder suspect or a hero. I'm afraid to let you out of my sight now."

Killian coughed and looked over at his grandfather. "It wouldn't have mattered in this case, would it?"

Thomas was quiet for a moment. "No, I wouldn't have stopped you."

Killian looked at Thomas intently. "Did we change the future? If I hadn't had that vision, the woman would have died."

"No, you didn't change anything since you didn't see her dead. This may be another gift shown to you."

That afternoon, they were sitting on the porch. Killian was feeling weak from smoke inhalation and enjoyed just sitting and breathing fresh air. He had bathed and changed his clothes so he didn't smell like smoke.

Killian remembered the letter from his father, and went inside to get it.

Dear Son,

We are so grateful that you sent the money. It saved us at a time when we needed it the most. Things are better here; we finally got rain so the crops are doing better. I was shocked when I found out you were in America. Maybe that is God's will. You say you knew why I didn't want you to go and now you know some people are deep-seated in their beliefs and it doesn't matter if you don't have special gifts; people will expect you to do things you cannot do. Give my regards to my father and brothers and write again soon. Papa

Killian looked at Thomas. "Papa doesn't believe in the power either." He gave the letter to his grandfather to read.

Killian closed his eyes, and he heard Thomas say, "Here comes the sheriff. I wonder what he wants now."

When the sheriff got there, he dismounted and walked up the steps. He nodded to Killian. "I want to thank you for saving my daughter's life today. I had you wrong. How did you know she went in there? It was an abandoned building, and she was trying to retrieve some old records."

Thomas looked at Killian to warn him to be careful how he answered. Killian thought for a moment. "I saw her go in on my way to the post office and when I came back, I was afraid she still might be in there, so I went in."

Thomas smiled because that was a good answer.

The sheriff smiled. "Well, no matter. I'm in your debt for saving her life. I'm going to the town council and see that you get recognition for this. Some type of medal or award and maybe a parade."

Killian froze, as did Thomas.

Killian looked up at the sheriff. "Sheriff, do I have a say-so in what I would like?"

"Why certainly. Anything you want."

"I would like nothing done. No awards, no parades, nothing. I think I did what any able-bodied man would do, and I don't think I should be rewarded for doing what God would expect me to do."

The sheriff frowned. "Yeah, but you're a hero. You got to realize that."

"You do what you want, but make sure you're doing it for me and not because you're grateful. You know my wishes, and I hope you'll respect them."

The sheriff scratched his head. "Well, OK, but I don't see why you…OK, that's the way it will be, but I am still in your debt."

"You owe me nothing."

The sheriff shook Killian's hand and left.

After the sheriff was out of hearing, Thomas looked at his grandson. "I think you have another gift revealed to us today."

Killian looked puzzled. "What is it?"

"The gift of wisdom. At eighteen, you show more wisdom and level-headedness than a man much older than your years."

Killian looked back at him. "I doubt that."

Thomas looked Killian in the eyes. "I can see it even if you can't. Trust me on these things, will you?"

Killian smiled and nodded. Killian was still not sure of his powers. He felt he had some powers, especially when a vision turned out to be real. He knew he could heal people, but he was scared of possessing those powers.

The following Wednesday night, Killian had another vision while he slept. He dreamed that he walked into a bedroom, and a woman was lying there dead. There was blood everywhere. Killian looked out the window and saw a train go by at high speed. The vision ended, and he woke with a start. He got out of bed, shook his grandfather awake, and told him of the vision.

Thomas looked concerned. "The train means it happens on a Thursday, so it must be this evening. You usually have these more on advance notice. I wonder why the change."

They got up and went out to the porch. When Thomas spotted Patrick leaving the barn, he waved him over. He told Patrick of the last two visions and what had happened in the burning building.

Thomas looked up at Patrick as he sat on his horse. "I'm worried that this has happened so soon. I may need you to verify that I was sick at dusk, and Killian came and got you, and we three were together until after the train went through."

Patrick agreed and rode off to work. The day went by, and there was no word of a murder. When Patrick came home that evening, he rode up and told Thomas that he had heard nothing. He suggested that it might just have been a bad dream.

Killian shook his head. "No, it was a vision, and I always wake up suddenly after I have them. It was no dream."

Patrick shrugged. "How do you explain that it didn't happen?"

Killian shrugged his shoulders also. Patrick left and went home.

It was Saturday when Thomas snapped his fingers. "I know what happened. You didn't have the vision a day late; you had it a week early. It will surely happen this Thursday. We'll have to get you out of town on some excuse."

Killian thought for a minute. "Don't you think this is going to bring attention to me if I leave town every time something like this happens?"

Thomas looked down at his boots, "Yeah, you're right. You see, you have wisdom. Can you think of anything?"

"Didn't you say the sheriff would be out of town next week?"

Thomas nodded.

"If I can push that hot-headed deputy into a fight, he may arrest me and put me in jail for the night. Think it's worth a try?"

Thomas smiled. "See, there you go again. Wisdom, I tell you."

That Thursday, Killian rode into town by himself. As he approached the sheriff's office, he saw the deputy talking to someone inside, and it looked as if he was just about to come out. Killian tied his horse up and walked down the boardwalk. He slowed as he got to the door, and sure enough, the deputy walked out, still looking back and talking. Killian ran into him. "Why don't you watch where you are going?"

The deputy pulled a gun out of his pocket and pointed it at Killian. "You're under arrest for assaulting a deputy of the law performing his official duties. Get inside."

Killian raised his hands. The deputy checked his pockets, opened a cell, and pushed Killian inside. Killian never took his eyes off the deputy, which unnerved the man. The deputy stepped up to the cell door. "Keep looking at me like that, and I'll keep you in here a month."

Killian kept on staring, and the deputy finally walked off. Killian could feel the fear in the deputy, and he grew bolder, knowing that he had that effect on people. He could sense fear and realized that his glare had powers that he didn't fully understand. "Why does my boldness, like staring, cause fear in people?" he asked himself.

Killian stayed in the cell the rest of the day, lying on the cot. The cell smelled dirty, and Killian saw a bug crawl across the floor every once in a while. He knew his grandfather wouldn't come into town to bail him out. He wondered about his uncles and their families. "Why are they opposed to helping a member of the family?"

He heard the train go through about dusk, and he slept very little that night, wondering if the murder had taken place. About eight o'clock Friday morning, someone came running to the jail to tell the deputy that there had been a murder. Killian knew it had happened, and his grandfather had been right.

About noon, his grandfather walked in. "I want my grandson out."

The deputy puffed out his chest. "He is being detained for assaulting an officer of the law in the performance of his duties."

"How long does he have to stay in jail for that?"

The deputy looked as official as he could. "I ain't decided yet, and I don't have time for this. I have a murder to investigate."

Thomas looked surprised. "Murder? Who was murdered?"

"Mr. Olson's wife. He found her dead this morning when he came in from the nightshift at the ironworks."

Thomas left, knowing that his grandson was safe. He went to the diner, got him a plate of food, and took it back to him. The deputy allowed him to give it to Killian.

Late that afternoon, the sheriff came running through the door. "What's this I hear about another murder?"

The deputy explained the whole story. The sheriff started to ask another question when he saw Killian in jail. "What's he in for?"

The deputy crossed his arms. "Assaulting an officer of the law in the—"

The sheriff interrupted him. "Never mind the official bullshit, just tell me what happened."

The deputy explained how Killian had run into him, and the sheriff looked up at the ceiling. "Bullshit. Let him out, now."

The deputy stood his ground. "He is also being held as a suspect in the murder of Mrs. Olson."

The sheriff narrowed his eyes. "When did you arrest him?"

"Yesterday about three o'clock."

The sheriff took a deep breath. "If he's been in jail all night, he couldn't have done it unless you helped him. Maybe I ought to lock you up as a suspect."

The deputy realized what he had done. He went over and unlocked the cell door. Killian came out, and the sheriff looked at him.

"I apologize for this. Tell your grandfather I'm sorry."

Killian nodded and looked at the deputy, who looked down at the floor to avoid Killian's stare. "Don't ever pull a gun on me again."

The sheriff looked at the deputy. "Gun…? OK, let's have it."

The deputy pulled the gun out of his pocket, and the sheriff put it in the desk drawer. He looked at the deputy. "You fool. You're lucky you didn't shoot your dick off."

Killian walked out as Thomas came riding up leading his horse.

As Killian mounted, the sheriff came out and apologized to Thomas.

Chapter 7

One night about midnight a week and a half later, Killian heard someone pounding on the door. He got up and saw his grandfather heading toward the door with a lamp. When he opened it, there stood Patrick. He almost screamed, "My little girl is burning up with a fever. My wife sent for the doctor but—" He looked at Killian and then at Thomas. "Can he come look at her?"

Thomas seemed to pause, but Killian threw on his clothes and followed Patrick out the door. "Let's go."

Thomas was dressing. "Go ahead. I'll be right behind you, but don't do anything until I get there."

Killian followed Patrick into his house. Patrick's wife was sitting in the rocking chair holding the ten-year-old girl. She was flushed, wet with sweat, and seemed unconscious. Patrick hesitated and then leaned down. "Linda, let Killian hold her."

"Why? What's he doing here?"

"Just let him see her."

"No, get out. I'll wait for the doctor."

Patrick reached down and took the little girl, but Linda was still holding on. Patrick shouted, "Let go! You're going to hurt her!"

Linda let go, tears streaming down her cheeks.

Thomas was there by then. He looked at Linda. "Go into the kitchen and make some coffee," he said.

She stood up and screamed, "Who wants coffee in the middle of the night?"

Thomas took her by the shoulders. "Go into the kitchen and make tea—anything—just go into the kitchen."

Patrick took her into the kitchen.

Killian took the child and held her. Her head was hot—not just from the fever but from the heat that only Killian could feel. He put his hand on her forehead. He could feel it getting hotter, and then it started getting cooler.

Linda was in the kitchen crying when the doctor came in. "She's burning up with a fever. She won't open her eyes." They rushed to the living room, and the little girl was sitting in Killian's lap. She was smiling and talking with Killian.

Linda came over. "What did you do to her?"

Thomas stepped up. "Nothing. He was just holding her, and her fever broke."

Linda turned and looked at them. "Two minutes ago, she seemed to be unconscious and wouldn't wake up. Now she's smiling and talking. What did you do to her?"

Thomas took the doctor by the arm. "She's a little hysterical. The child will be all right, but examine her, if you would."

The doctor felt the little girl's head, looked down her throat, took her temperature, and listened to her chest. "If she had a fever, she doesn't have one now. There's nothing I can do."

Thomas patted the doctor on the back. "I thank you for coming. How much is an emergency house call?"

The doctor looked at everyone suspiciously. "Two dollars." Thomas gave him three, and he left.

Linda put the child to bed and returned to the parlor as Killian and Thomas were about to leave. She faced them. "OK, you three. What happened here tonight?"

Patrick looked at his wife. "Woman, the child is well. What do you care how it happened or who did it? Be thankful she's OK."

"I'm not buying this. I want to know why, when our daughter looked like she was near death, you ran for Killian?"

Patrick stammered a bit. "She wasn't as bad as we thought and—"

"Don't tell me that. I'm not stupid!" Linda screamed.

Killian walked over to her and looked her in the eyes. "Go to bed and speak of this to no one." His voice and his look made her draw back. Killian felt her fear. She turned, went into the child's room, and lay down with her.

When Killian and Thomas were on the porch and Thomas was shutting the door behind them, they heard Linda say, "What if I do speak of this? What can they do?"

Patrick's voice carried through the wall. "If you do, and she comes down sick again, you'd better get the doctor, because he won't be back. That goes for any of our family. Do you want to take that chance of one of them dying because of you?"

Linda was quiet for a moment. "No. I won't say anything, but I would like an explanation of what went on here."

"Maybe someday, but it's for our own good that you don't know right now."

Thomas looked at Killian and motioned for them to leave.

The next morning, Patrick rode over. "We need to think about telling Linda. I'm not sure she won't swear the other women to secrecy and discuss it with them."

Thomas nodded. "The more people that know, the more dangerous it is for Killian. But I guess I would rather one more know than five more. Let me talk to her."

Patrick nodded and then turned his horse and rode off to the ironworks.

No sooner was he out of sight, than they saw Linda come out the door and start toward them. Killian got up and went inside. When Linda got to Thomas's porch, she looked hard at her father-in-law. "Grandpa, I need to know. This is scaring me."

Thomas sat silently for a moment. "I'll tell you, but if you tell one living soul, you could cause Killian's death."

She looked away and then back at Thomas. "I don't understand this whole situation. You took him in, and you've never done that for any relative. You made them stay with one of us until they could afford a place of their own. He doesn't work. You don't let him out of your sight. He scares me when he tells me to do something. I'm scared not to do it. The look in his eyes frightens me, and I don't know why."

Thomas put his hand on her shoulder. "Have you heard of the seventh son of the seventh son?"

"Yes, but I don't believe any of that's true."

Thomas just sat there and stared at her.

She finally shook her head with a skeptical look. "Are you telling me he healed her by just holding her and touching her?"

Thomas answered slowly. "Do you believe that?"

She looked away and put her head in her hands. "I saw it happen, but I still can't believe that a human being has that power."

Thomas looked off down the road. "It happened. You saw it happen. Now the danger is, if you tell anyone, there will be a line of people on one side that will stretch back to New York wanting to be cured of hangnails and another line of people wanting to hang him for witchcraft. If that happens, he won't be here the next time one of your children is near death. Do you understand? Talk with Patrick about it, please."

She nodded, and tears welled up in her eyes. "I thought he only had four brothers."

Thomas shook his head. "He has six, just like your husband. The only difference is, Paddy is the oldest, and Killian is the youngest."

She nodded, got up, and left.

A few days later, Thomas and Killian were riding down to look at the ironworks. As they passed the store in town, a beautiful, redheaded girl about Killian's age came out. "How're you doing, Mr. O'Rourke?"

"Fine, fine, Molly. How are you today? Oh, Molly McGuire, this is my grandson, Killian. Killian, Molly."

Killian looked down from his horse. "It's a pleasure to meet you, Molly."

Molly did a small curtsy. "The pleasure is all mine. I've heard you were in town, fresh from Ireland. I can tell, because you haven't lost any of your accent like most of the Irish here—including myself, of course."

Killian smiled. "I've been trying because when I was in New York, it started a fight when I spoke."

She laughed heartily. "It's a little better here. There are some, but there are so many Irish here, most don't say much. Well, I must be going. I hope you will call on me sometime and tell me the latest about Ireland. Good day."

Killian bowed a little. "And a very good day it is."

She smiled and walked away.

Thomas cut his eyes at Killian. "Now, now. You don't have time for romance, and besides, she is spoken for by a big Scotsman named David McCall."

Killian smiled. "She didn't ask me to come marry her. She just asked me to call so we can discuss recent events in Ireland." Killian thought she was the most beautiful girl he had ever seen.

Thomas rode on. "You still don't have time."

"Why not? I have nothing but time."

Thomas looked at him and said no more. He admired the logic and common sense this eighteen-year-old had. They arrived at the ironworks, got off their horses, and walked in. They found Patrick in the office as well as his brother Dermit, who lived across the road from Patrick.

"How are things going here?" Thomas asked.

Patrick gave a look to Killian. "We are shorthanded since Dean is laid up with his knee. I don't know when he'll be back, if he'll be back."

Thomas shook his head. "If he wasn't such a hothead, he wouldn't have a hurt knee. Replace him with someone else."

"What do we do about his pay? He has a family, you know."

"Pay him out of my share and leave him at home."

Thomas showed Killian around the ironworks. They stopped by a big office with twenty people at desks. Thomas went in, and when Killian followed him, he noticed the stifling heat in the room. The office manager came over. "What can I do for you today, Mr. O'Rourke?"

Thomas explained that he was showing his grandson around. The man shook Killian's hand. "Do you have any questions I can answer?"

Killian looked over the room. "Why is it so hot in here?"

The man smiled and crossed his arms. "Well, it's just that time of year. We can't do anything about that, can we?"

Killian stared at him and knew that unnerved the man. "Why not open the windows? You have three on this wall, three on that one, and four in the back."

The man looked at Thomas. "I find that it distracts them when the windows are open."

Killian looked at the workers. Their hair was matted down with sweat.

He walked over and opened a window. Cool, fresh air flowed into the room. He opened the next two and looked back, pointing at a man sitting there. "Open the rest of the windows," he said.

The man jumped up. "Yes, sir."

Killian saw the relief on the workers' faces and the thanks in their smiles.

The office manager looked at Thomas for help. "Sir, I must protest. I am held responsible for the work this group produces."

Killian gave him that look. "You don't think they'll be more productive if they are more comfortable?" He stared at the man for a moment. "Leave the windows up while it's this hot. You can close them this fall or when it rains."

The man looked imploringly at Thomas, but he said nothing.

"Don't look at him; look at me," Killian said. "Do you understand me about the windows?"

The man was shaken. "Well, yes, sir." He shot another quick look at Thomas as Killian walked out the door.

As they walked through the plant, Thomas looked over at him. "I think what you did was right, but what gives you any authority here?"

Killian kept walking. "My birthright."

Thomas didn't reply, but he liked this boldness and character in Killian.

Killian wondered where the boldness came from. He figured it was part of being the seventh son of the seventh son, but why was he just now feeling it in America?

That evening, as they sat on the front porch, they saw Linda and Patrick walking toward them. Patrick propped one foot on the bottom step. "Mr. Stout came into my office raising Cain about Killian telling him to keep the windows open. I generally let him run his department without interference." He looked at Killian and then at Thomas.

Killian spoke first. "It's eighty-five degrees outside, and keeping the windows shut makes it close to one hundred in there. Those people will be a lot more productive if they don't have sweat running off them. Maybe you should go down and interfere more often in that department. Opening the windows will double their work output."

Patrick gave Killian a sidelong glance. "I suppose that's true, but what I'm asking is what gives you the authority to come into my plant and make decisions like that?"

Thomas spoke up. "That's not your plant. It's my plant, and his birthright gives him the authority."

Patrick glared at his father. "You're not serious, are you?"

Thomas glared back. "Do I look serious?"

"Papa, may I talk with you in the house?"

Thomas walked into the house with Patrick. That left Linda out there with Killian, and she was obviously nervous. Killian tried to calm her down, asking, "How's the little girl?"

Linda smiled as she looked up. "She's fine. I never did thank you for that," she said, and then she looked down at the ground again and rubbed the fingers on her right hand.

"It's not necessary to thank me. What's wrong with your hand?"

"Oh, I have rheumatism in my fingers. Pains me sometimes."

"Let me see it."

She held out her hand, and he took it. He put his right hand on top of it and his left hand underneath.

She frowned. "It seems to be getting warm, hot almost."

"It will go away soon." When he felt no more heat, he released her hand.

She had no more pain. She frowned at him again, moving her fingers back and forth.

"You still don't believe in me, do you?"

She looked down. "I do now. How did you…never mind. Thanks." She smiled at him.

Killian smiled back, and that seemed to put her at ease. He found he could influence people with a smile also. He made a mental note to remember that.

About that time, Patrick came out the door. "Let's go." They walked away without saying anything.

Killian asked, "How's Patrick doing?"

"He understands less than I do. I don't know why I let you do that today, but I know it was right."

"Yes, sir. It was."

Thomas said with a smile, "Are you taking over the holdings from me?"

Killian laughed. "No, sir. You're the family patriarch, and if you tell me I can't do something, I'll not do it. How are you going to leave it when you die?"

Thomas thought for a moment. "I am going to have all the holdings run by a six-man board made up of your uncles."

"You think they will run it as successfully as you have?"

"More and more that seems unlikely, but I have no choice."

The next day, Killian and Thomas were riding down the street and stopped in at the market run by another uncle. Thomas dismounted.

"I need to speak to my son. This won't take long."

"How about I walk down the street to the general store? We need a few things at the house."

Thomas nodded. "That's a good idea. When I finish, I'll come down there."

Killian walked down the street, and when he got to the store, he ran into Molly. "Oh, I'm sorry. I didn't realize you lived here," Killian said, holding the door open for her.

She laughed real big. "It seems like it, doesn't it? I'm in here three or four times a week."

Killian smiled. "Well, in that case, I'll try to come here more often so I may accidently run into you."

Molly blushed. "You don't have to see me by accident. Call on me. I would love to sit down and talk with you."

Killian looked into her green eyes. "Well, my grandfather says you are spoken for by a big Scotsman. I wouldn't want to cause problems."

Molly frowned at him. "I've heard that before, but I'm not spoken for by any man, at least not at the present."

"Great. Then we can sit down and talk. I just passed a park. Can you walk there and talk for a while?" Killian offered her his arm.

"Most assuredly." She took his arm, and they walked down to a grove where there were picnic tables. Killian chose one under a tree that shaded the area. He faced her and took a good look at her. Her hair was as red as his was, and her complexion looked like silk. Her green eyes were intoxicating. She had on a green-plaid dress that swept the ground.

"Well, Molly McGuire, what do you do when you're not going to the store?"

She smiled as she folded her hands on the table. "Well, I teach school and…oh, that reminds me. Did you go to the ironworks and make the office manager raise the windows yesterday?"

Killian frowned. "Wow, that has spread fast. How did you find out?"

She laughed. "My father works there as an accountant and said you saved his life—everybody's really. He said he couldn't see the ledger sheet for the sweat in his eyes."

"Well, it seemed like it made sense. Everybody is more productive if they are as comfortable as they can get."

"That's it exactly, but old Mr. Stout doesn't see that. He likes to see people suffer."

Killian changed the subject. "Well, you teach school. I bet that takes up a lot of time."

"Yes, if you consider grading papers and making lesson plans. Tell me about Ireland. I left there years ago as a young child, but I'd love to go back for a visit. What's it like?"

"It was pretty bad when I left. We were in a drought. There weren't enough jobs for everyone, and a lot of people were going hungry. I dug potatoes for twelve hours a day for ten shillings."

"How much is ten shillings in American money?"

"About fifty cents."

"You did that for twelve hours?"

"It was the only job I could get. I talked my papa into letting me go to the coast to look for a job. A man paid my fare over here, and here I am."

"Did you leave your papa and mama over there?"

"I left me papa and…four brothers there. My mama died a year ago."

Molly hesitated, and then said, "Oh, I'm sorry. What do you do now?"

Killian had to think fast. "My grandfather is taking me around to decide where I might fit in with the family business. I have six uncles here, so I might work for one of them."

"Six uncles? Your grandmother had six children? How many boys and how many girls?"

Killian smiled and looked down. "She had seven boys, including my papa. No girls."

"And you have four brothers. Any sisters?"

"No, all boys again."

"So you're with your grandfather most of the day?"

"It seems so. At least lately. I live with him. My uncles have their own houses."

Molly was taken with Killian. "Do you miss your brothers and father?"

"I really miss me father, but all my brothers are married, and we used to fight a lot, so it's kind of nice not having them around. Why are you laughing?"

"You said 'me father.' I haven't heard that in a while."

Killian was embarrassed. "I'm really trying to not say that. It just slips out sometimes."

Molly smiled again. "Well, I think it's cute when you say it."

Killian blushed and smiled as he looked away. "Do you teach all the grades in school?"

"Oh yes. I have four first-graders, four second-graders, no third-graders. Let's see, I have two fifth-graders and one sixth-grader, so I teach them together; three in seventh, two in eighth, and one in ninth. None in tenth through twelfth. They usually drop out to go to work and help the family."

"That's what happened to me. I got through the tenth, but never finished the last two grades. Say, maybe I could come to class and be your eleventh and twelfth grade."

She raised her eyes. "When did you finish the tenth?"

"Two years ago."

"Why did you finish so late? Did you repeat any grades?"

"No, I completed them all. I started when I was six."

She smiled. "That would make you eighteen years old, silly."

"What's wrong with being eighteen years old?"

She looked surprised. "Wait, I'm confused. How old are you now?"

Killian looked at her, confused also. "Eighteen. I thought we'd covered that."

She raised her pretty, red eyebrows. "Eighteen? Really? I thought you were…my age."

"Is it permissible to ask your age?"

She looked away and smiled. "I'm twenty."

He smiled at her. "I thought you were my age. Of course, I'll be nineteen in about nine months."

She laughed aloud at that.

"Would you seriously come to school to complete the last two years?"

"Yeah, I would. I need to finish."

"I think that's great. What if you get a job?"

"I could take time for school, I'm sure."

"I would love to have you. Can you start this fall?"

"Let me run it by my grandfather before I give you the final say-so."

Suddenly, a voice behind Killian roared, "Who are you, and what are you doing talking to my girl?"

Before he could turn around, Molly jumped up. "David McCall, I am not your girl. I'll decide whose girl I am when the time comes, and I want you to quit telling people that."

Killian stood up. David was about four inches taller than he was, and he was big—big and fat. He tried to hide it by wearing his shirt out and pulling his belt about three notches tighter than it should have been. David looked at Killian. "What are you doing here?"

Killian calmly looked up at him. "Enrolling in school," he said.

That made Molly laugh.

David stepped up to him. "If I catch you around her again, I'll knock you out. Do you understand that?" He drew back his fist.

"Yes, do you mean like this?"

Killian slugged David in the nose, and he fell straight back. He didn't move. People started gathering around and, all of a sudden, Thomas was standing there.

Thomas looked at him. "I figured if there was a crowd, you'd be somewhere in the middle of it. What happened here?"

"Well, he said he was going to knock me out, so I beat him to the punch."

Thomas grabbed his shirt and said, "Let's get out of here." Killian turned to Molly, but she was gone.

When Thomas and Killian had started for home, Thomas said, "What were you doing talking to Molly McGuire?"

"I ran into her at the store, and we went and sat down to talk. She wants me to enroll in school and finish the last two grades I didn't finish."

"You're not serious, are you?"

"Yes, sir, I'm serious. Do you have something against education?"

"No, not in general, but aren't you a little old to be going to school with all those little kids?"

"It will be awkward, but school is important to me."

Thomas smiled. "I wonder if it's school or Molly McGuire that's important to you."

Killian smiled back. "A little of both, I suppose."

Thomas liked the fact that Killian didn't back down when it concerned something he wanted.

They arrived back at home, and Thomas handed his reins to Killian. "Take care of the horses," he said.

Killian took the reins of Thomas's mount and rode over to the barn that Thomas and Patrick shared. He unsaddled the horses, fed them, and hooked the rope across the stall. When he turned, Patrick was standing there.

"I really don't like what you did yesterday at the ironworks," Patrick said. "You had no authority to do what you did."

"Do you think it's right to make those people suffer because the boss likes to be sadistic?"

"No, I don't. I don't have a problem with what you did. The problem I have is you're doing it with no authority."

"I saw a situation that needed immediate correction. You're the boss. You should have prevented it from happening in the first place. I think that's what's bothering you."

"Where was Papa when you did that?"

"Standing right there beside me. Why?"

Patrick turned red. "You mean he didn't stop you?"

"No, he didn't. He knew I was right. He expressed his concern over my making that move, but he knew it was the right decision. The proper procedure would have been to bring that to your attention and let you correct it."

"That's right. Why didn't you?"

"Because the situation needed immediate attention. In this case, doing right trumped procedure. It should never have happened in the first place, but that falls on you because you're the boss. That man works for you, and everything he does reflects on you."

Killian stood silent, waiting for Patrick to make the next move.

Finally, Patrick looked at him with a serious face. "Papa said that it was your birthright to do that. Does that mean because you are the seventh son of the seventh son, you have the right to do things that undermine my authority?"

Killian tried to choose his next words carefully. "No, it means that as the seventh son of the seventh son, things are sometimes revealed to me that others fail to see, for whatever reason. In this case, you relied on a man who made the wrong decision. It was not my intention to undermine you or embarrass you."

Patrick stood there for a moment and then turned and walked off. Killian hated to get crossways with Patrick, but he felt he was right. He walked back to the house and went in. Thomas was sitting at the table.

"Come on and eat before it gets cold. What took you so long?"

"Patrick and I had a discussion about the ironworks incident. Evening, Gretchen. How are you?"

She smiled and nodded an OK.

Thomas raised his eyebrows. "Well, who convinced who about who was wrong?"

Killian sat down. "He didn't convince me I was wrong. I don't know if I convinced him of anything or not." They finished eating, both thinking about the incident.

The next day, Thomas said, "I need to go back to the ironworks, but I am afraid to take you."

Killian smiled. "I'll stay here. Can you risk leaving me alone?"

"No. Go get the horses."

Killian brought the horses around, and Thomas was waiting for him. They rode off to the ironworks. As they rode up to the plant, Killian noticed that all of the windows in the administration building were down.

He kept his eyes on the building. "Excuse me a minute, Grandpa." He rode across the grass to the building. He stopped and looked into the room. The manager saw him and must have said something because three men got up and opened the windows. Killian sat there a minute and stared at him, and then he rode back over to Thomas.

Thomas said nothing. They walked in and climbed the stairs to Patrick's office on the second floor. As they walked down the hall, they heard Patrick say, "What were the damn windows doing closed anyway? It's too damn hot. If you can't run that office without me checking on you, then I'll get someone who can. Do you understand me?"

Apparently, Mr. Stout nodded, because they heard nothing else. The man came out and almost ran into Killian. Killian stood his ground and made the man walk around him.

They went into Patrick's office and Patrick looked perturbed. "Did you say something to him again?"

Thomas answered for Killian. "He didn't interfere. The man saw us coming down the road and knew he was caught, so he came running to you. Now, I want to know what the problem is in the furnace room."

Killian walked over to the door and went out into the hall, where he could overlook the work being done on the floor below. He stood at the rail and watched so Thomas could keep an eye on him. He felt every employee's eyes on him. It was as if they were silently pleading for help, but he knew he shouldn't cross Patrick, if possible.

Thomas came out and said, "Follow me."

They went downstairs and into the furnace room. It was extremely hot in there from the molten material they were pouring from giant cauldrons. Thomas stood there, and the workers looked at him, but said nothing. Thomas leaned over where Killian could hear him above the noise. "These people are asking for more money because of the heat."

Killian looked at Thomas. "Give it to them."

Thomas turned to him. "I pay all my workers the same. It keeps down the squabbling."

"Apparently not. Do you have a lot of men asking for this job?"

"Hell, no. We have to make them work in here. Anybody that screws up their regular job gets put in here."

"Pay them more than men who are working in better conditions and you'll have a list of people wanting this job. Quit using this important step in the process as punishment. Two problems solved. This is like the windows being down when it's hot."

Thomas knew that Killian wasn't making a suggestion, but rather giving a direction to him. He saw the reasoning in that and was smiling on the inside. He turned, and they went back to the office. When they got to Patrick's office door, Thomas put his hand on Killian's shoulder. "Wait here for a minute."

Thomas went in, shut the door, and stood there talking to Patrick. Patrick seemed concerned and looked through the window at Killian briefly. Thomas came back out. "We've done all the damage we can do here today. Let's go."

As they rode back through town, Killian saw Molly walking down the street. He looked at Thomas and said, "Grandpa, I'll be a minute."

He rode over to her. She stopped, and he got down off his horse. "You left yesterday, and I didn't get to say good-bye."

She looked determined. "I don't approve of fighting, by anyone."

Killian looked at her. "You can't be Irish if you don't like to fight."

She couldn't help but smile.

"Still, I don't approve of one human perpetrating violence against another."

"Now you sound like a schoolteacher."

She smiled again.

He continued, "Besides, that's easy for you to say because you're a woman and didn't have to fight…four brothers for a place at the table. I suppose I should have let him hit me, and then you would be mad at him and not me."

She shook her head. "I'm mad at both of you. You should go to him and ask for forgiveness."

Killian looked her in the eye. "Even you should know, in your sheltered little world, that if you put an Irishman and a Scotsman within striking distance of one another, one of them is going to swing. I won't be bothering you again." He turned to walk off.

"Killian, wait."

He turned back.

"This won't stop you from coming to school, will it?" She gave him a weak smile.

He looked at her for a second and nodded. "Yes," he replied. He turned, mounted his horse, and rode back to where Thomas was sitting on his horse on the other side of the street. They rode off with Molly standing there watching. Killian said to himself, "I like this girl. I like her a lot, but she is too unreasonable."

Thomas broke the silence. "You and your girlfriend have a tiff?" He smiled.

Killian kept a straight face. "She's not my girlfriend. I can't see how anyone can be that narrow-minded."

Thomas reached over and put his hand on Killian's shoulder. "Let me tell you something. If you think your powers will win out over a woman, they won't. There's nothing as powerful as the ways of a woman."

Killian looked at his grandfather, and he was smiling. Killian broke into a smile too.

They rode back to the house and left the horses at the hitching rail. They went in, and Gretchen had made them lunch. Afterward, they went back to their rocking chair thrones on the front porch.

Killian sat there looking down the street. "Gretchen is nice. How long have you been married?"

"About five years. I needed someone to keep house, and she needed a place because her husband died. He was a good friend of mine, and she was going to be out on the curb. We married so the town gossips wouldn't start. You see, she has her own bedroom, and I have mine."

103

Killian nodded.

Thomas added, "If anything happens to me, make sure she's not put out on the curb, please."

Killian nodded. "She's family. She'll be taken care of like family. I can promise you that."

"Thank you."

At that time, they saw a one-horse cart coming up the street.

Thomas squinted. "That looks like your girlfriend. Maybe she's come to ask your forgiveness or convince you to ask for hers." He winked at Killian. As she pulled up, Thomas added, "If you'll excuse me for a few minutes." He got up and walked in the house.

Killian nodded his head. "Top of the day to you, Miss McGuire."

She looked at him. "Are we going to be formal with each other or civil?"

"Civil, of course," Killian answered. "Won't you come up and have a seat?"

She walked up and sat in Thomas's rocker. "I hope your grandfather didn't leave on my account."

"No, he said he had something to take care of, but I'm sure he was just being courteous."

Molly smiled and shifted in Thomas's chair. "Look, I want to apologize for my actions and attitude. You're right. You didn't have a choice with David. Had you backed down, he would have proclaimed you a coward, so you did the only thing you could do and that was to hit him first. He's a bully."

"Thank you for seeing it for what it was."

"Will you reconsider coming to school?"

Killian looked off. "I'll come to school to see you and maybe learn something on the side about math and American history."

She smiled again. "That'll be fine. I'll see that you learn."

"Wait a minute. I just thought of a reason not to go to school. Will a student seeing a teacher socially be allowed?"

"Would an eighteen-year-old student be interested in a twenty-year-old teacher, socially?"

"This eighteen-year-old already is. I might walk you home after school and carry your books."

She leaned closer to Killian. "That would be nice. I really must go. It's been nice talking with you."

"Can I call on you sometime?"

"Yes. Do you know where I live?"

"No, but I bet I can find out." Killian walked her out to her cart and opened the door for her. She got in and sat down. She picked up the reins and looked Killian in the eye. Killian held her gaze.

She looked at him for a few minutes. "Why is it that when I look into your green eyes, I feel there is a deep secret in there?"

Killian smiled. "Because there is. I can't tell you what it is. You'll have to discover that on your own."

She couldn't help but smile as she drove away. Killian wondered what she saw.

Thomas came back after she left. "Well, did you iron out your differences?" he asked.

Killian nodded, contentment on his face. "Oh yeah, we're doing fine. I think I'll try to finish those two grades this fall, though. How do you feel about escorting me to school?"

Thomas smiled. "I'll probably let you go alone."

They saw Patrick ride up the street from work, and he came up to the hitching rail and tied his horse up. "We have a family problem," he said to Thomas. He looked at Killian and then back at Thomas.

Thomas nodded and said, "He's family; go ahead."

Patrick looked down at the ground. "Dean thinks his wife, Alberta, is seeing someone else."

"Why does he think that?" Thomas asked.

"He said one of his friends saw her horse and buggy over past the stockyards."

Killian frowned. "Was she driving it?"

Patrick nodded. "She was seen coming out of a house and getting into it."

"What night was it?"

"Thursday night. She's supposed to be going over to Mrs. Bea's for quilting. She's been doing that for years, but Mrs. Bea doesn't live anywhere near the stockyards."

Killian asked, "Has anybody ever seen one of her quilts?"

Thomas looked at Patrick, and Patrick looked back at Killian. "Come to think of it, I haven't. In fact, she was over last winter to borrow a quilt." Patrick looked at them. "What do we do? Confront her?"

No one spoke, so Killian smiled. "I would think we should stay out of those types of problems unless asked."

Patrick was getting frustrated. "Dean came to me and asked what he should do."

Killian suppressed a smile. "Then help him, but it's a job for you to handle."

Thomas smiled. "I agree. But still, I want to have a family meeting here next Thursday night. Tell everyone it's mandatory. Quilts be damned."

Patrick started to walk away. "I'll spread the word. I have a friend who delivers the mail out in that neighborhood she was seen in. Maybe I could ask who lives in the house she went to."

Killian looked at Patrick. "You're the one he asked for help. If you think that might help you, you'll have to decide."

Thomas smiled again.

Patrick stopped before he got to his horse. "You two aren't going to help me on this, are you?"

They both laughed, and Killian shook his head. "We don't have the expertise that you do."

Patrick laughed as he mounted his horse and rode toward the barn.

The next Thursday, each family brought homemade cookies and cakes, and the men had some Irish whiskey. When they were gathered in the big room downstairs in Thomas's house that was built for such occasions, Thomas stood up. "I would like my six sons and my grandson to take their places up front, please."

Dean asked, "Why does he get to come up front?"

Thomas took a deep breath before responding. "He represents my seventh son and because I said so."

Killian knew that his uncles didn't want to fight him and that they knew that Thomas would back him. He went up immediately, knowing that something in his inner being gave him the right to be there. That inner strength empowered him, but it also alienated his uncles and their families.

"Now, we all know there have been three unsolved murders in the area. From this point, I don't want any women going anywhere by themselves. Always go at least in pairs and preferably three or more. I don't want to hear that you don't have anyone to go with. If that happens, I'll send Killian with you. Are there any questions?"

He waited for a response and got none. "Then everybody have fun fellowshipping."

Everybody knew there had better not be any questions. Grandpa's word was law in the O'Rourke family. You followed it or left the family.

Killian walked over to Patrick as he took a shot of Irish whiskey. "Which one is Alberta?"

"The dark-haired one in the yellow dress."

Killian asked, "Is she blind?"

"No, of course not. Why do you ask?"

"Oh, I don't know. Since she married Dean, I thought—"

Patrick laughed.

Killian went out on the front porch to make room in the house. Dean and Alberta came out, and Dean shot him a dirty look as he walked on crutches, but Alberta stopped and put her hand on Killian's shoulder to balance herself while she fixed her shoe.

She pulled her shoe off and put it back on. "I hate to miss quilting Thursday."

Killian felt as if pins were sticking into his shoulder while she had her hand on it. When she finished talking, the feeling stopped. Killian looked up at her and knew she was lying.

After everyone left, he went to his grandfather and told him what had happened. "Another gift you have. The ability to tell when people are telling the truth. We do need to do something about Alberta, but I don't know what."

Killian thought for a minute. "Let me get someone else to handle it."

"But who?"

"Patrick's wife. She'll know how to handle it, but let me talk to her."

The next day after all the uncles had left for work, Killian was thinking about Dean and Alberta. He felt something within telling him to do something about it. He walked over to see Linda. He knocked on the door.

She smiled when she saw him. "Come in," she said.

Killian looked down at his dusty boots. "Perhaps you can step out."

She did, asking, "What can I do for you?"

"Did Patrick tell you that we believe Alberta is seeing another man?"

Her mouth dropped as she took on a look of disbelief. "No, he certainly did not. I can't believe that. When would she have time? She's at home, at church, or quilting."

"Have you ever seen a quilt?"

She looked at him with a blank stare. "No, I haven't."

Killian looked at her. "Someone told Dean she was seen at a house over beyond the stockyards on Thursday night. Patrick checked with someone he knows, and a Mr. Belker lives there. He's a widower and pretty well off. Maybe it's the money."

Linda looked at him in disbelief. "Is Dean still getting paid by the ironworks?"

"It is sent to him by the ironworks, but Grandpa is paying him. Do you know Alberta well enough to have a talk with her?"

"Sure. We've been friends since childhood, and we're the same age. I can talk to her, but how am I going to tell her I know?"

"That's why I told Grandpa that I wanted you to do it. You'll find a way that none of us could."

Linda nodded and went back inside her house as Killian left.

Three days later, Linda came over after dark and said to Killian, "Can I talk to you?"

Killian stepped out on the porch.

"I went to her and asked if I could go to quilting with her. She told me I wouldn't like it and tried to discourage me. I told her that it was OK for her to go to quilting as long as she didn't go anywhere else. She was shocked and asked me what I was referring to, and I told her that I thought she knew what I was saying. Then I told her that if she was going to continue to go to quilting, she'd better bring home a quilt soon. She asked me if I had talked to Dean. I told her I didn't, but someone told him she had been seen in the area of the stockyards. She lowered her head and got tears in her eyes. She just nodded her head and went back home. Before she left, I told her if she needed to go for a last good-bye visit to take me with her for safety. She just nodded, but hasn't said anything else."

Killian nodded and smiled at her. "You did well."

She started to walk away, but stopped. "Can I ask you a question?"

Killian nodded.

"Why is it that when I look at you, I see an eighteen-year-old boy, but when you speak, I feel I'm talking to a forty-year-old man? Is it part of being the seventh son of the seventh son?"

Killian nodded, patted her on the shoulder, and went back in. She went home.

Killian could feel a knowledge and wisdom envelop him at times, and he wondered why he thought certain thoughts.

Chapter 8

A few nights later, Killian had another vision. He saw people crying and holding each other. Some had blood on them, and their clothes were torn. He saw a train off the track. Some of the cars were turned over and burning. Then he woke up. He went to Thomas's bed and told him about the vision.

Thomas sat up in bed. "There's nothing to do but stay away from the train tracks," he said. Four days later, word came that a train had derailed fifty miles south of Knoxville. There were six dead from the city, and there were funerals for those who were from Knoxville. In his vision, Killian had seen men and women crying at the funerals.

The next day, Killian rode to the store to pick up some things Gretchen needed. On the way back, he passed Dean's house. He saw Dean lying on the ground beside the porch. He quickly rode over, got off his horse, and looked at him. Dean seemed to have fallen and was unconscious. He had a cut and a bump on his head. Killian started to see if he could get Dean to respond, but a thought hit him. "Why not see if I can help Dean's knee?"

He pulled Dean's pants leg up above the knee. He placed both of his hands on Dean's knee. He could feel the heat; it was almost too hot to touch. "The injury must really be severe," he thought. Dean moaned, and Killian hoped he wouldn't wake up before the heat disappeared. Finally, the knee seemed to cool down. He pulled the pants leg down and patted Dean on the face.

Dean opened his eyes. "What happened?" he asked.

"I was riding by and saw you lying here. You must have fallen off the porch and hit your head."

Dean touched his head. "I remember now. I was trying to mount my horse and my knee pained me so bad, I fell."

Killian looked down behind the house and saw the horse out in the pasture, grazing.

"Just lie here a minute while I go get your horse." He mounted up, rode into the pasture, picked up the horse's reins, and led it back. When he got back, Dean was walking around. Killian asked, "How's the head?"

Dean was looking at his leg. "What? Oh, the head. It's fine, but my knee doesn't hurt now. I don't understand it."

"It was probably out of joint and the fall knocked it back in, don't you think?"

"Yeah, that must be it." He took his horse's reins and looked up at Killian. "Thanks for stopping and seeing to me. I thought you would have left me here."

Killian smiled. "No, I wouldn't do that to anybody. Have a good day." He rode off. When he got to the house, Thomas came out on the porch and sat down. Killian told him what he had done.

Thomas slowly nodded. "Thanks; he needs all the help he can get. That knee paining him like it did made him almost impossible to live with." Killian figured his grandfather was making excuses for Alberta.

That afternoon, before Patrick came home, they saw Linda and Alberta walking toward them. Thomas shook his head. "This can't be good."

When they got there, it was obvious that Linda was leading Alberta. Linda stopped halfway up the steps and looked at them. "Killian, Berta saw you heal Dean's knee. She was afraid you were into devil worship and stealing his soul. I had to tell her the truth before she said something to someone else. We're fortunate that we're not only sisters-in-law but best friends too. I think she should hear it from you."

Thomas stood up. "Come up here and sit down, Berta."

She sat in his chair, and Killian got up out of his. Thomas sat down so he could talk to Alberta. "Look at me. Do you know the story of the seventh son of the seventh son?"

She shook her head.

Thomas continued, "Legend has it that the seventh son of the seventh son has unusual gifts. I believe these gifts are ordained by God. Killian has the gift of healing, among others. We keep it a secret because some people will react like you did and think it's devil worship. When he came here, that first murder occurred and the sheriff suspected him because he was new to the community. Had they known he was the seventh son of the seventh son, many would have reacted like you did, and he would have been hanged. Do you understand why it's important that you not tell anyone? Not even Dean."

She thought a minute and then nodded.

Alberta smoothed her apron. "I thought he only had four brothers."

"No, that's a story we made up so no one would figure it out. His life is in the hands of all who know. The fewer people know, the safer he is. That's why we have only revealed it when necessary." He continued, "Think about this and come back with any questions you might have. Killian and I will be glad to talk this out with you. We want you to fully understand that one word, just one word may get him hanged or run out of town."

Linda took her by the shoulders and led her back home. Killian watched them walk away. "You think we will be OK?" he asked Thomas.

Thomas sighed. "I hope so. I would hate to have to kill her."

Killian looked at Thomas to see if he was serious but he couldn't tell, so he said nothing.

Chapter 9

It was a few weeks later when Alberta came over early one morning to see Thomas. "I need to go to Seymour and see my mother. I got a letter saying she was extremely ill. Can I go by myself?"

Thomas shook his head. "No! Is there someone who can go with you?"

"We have several sick, and Linda is filling in for them at the market. There's no one."

Thomas looked off as he pondered for a few minutes. "Tell Dean he can take off at the ironworks and go with you."

Tears filled her eyes. "He was the first one I asked, and he said he couldn't get off. If you make him go, it will only make things worse between us." She crossed her arms and dabbed at the tears with a handkerchief.

"Things are bad between you?"

She nodded.

Thomas looked down the street. "Seymour is what…three days' horse ride?"

Again, she nodded. "I'll have Killian go with you, and you both should take a bedroll in case you can't find a boardinghouse along the way. I'll have Gretchen make up some food to go with you. Does the train go near there?"

She nodded. "It goes southeast, but you can't take the horses, so you have a two-day walk to Momma's house. Hardly seems worth it."

Thomas nodded and said, "Go pack some clothes. You can leave right away." She turned and left.

Thomas fetched a ground cloth and two blankets and rolled them up. He also brought out a set of saddlebags and a canteen. He found Killian in the kitchen and told him what he was going to have to do. He gave him the saddlebags. "Pack your clothes in one side and put the food in the other. It will be ready in a minute. I would send you in a carriage, but Dean told me there was a shortcut across country that a carriage can't do."

Killian got everything ready and put his saddlebags on the horse, tying them to the saddle. He placed the bedroll behind the saddle. He mounted up, and as he started to go, Thomas touched his hand. "You know not to touch anyone unless it is life or death, and even then, make a wise decision. I feel good, knowing you will know what to do and when to do it. If her mother is near death, let her die. She's an old woman anyway."

Killian nodded and rode over to Alberta's. She was struggling to get the saddle on, and sweat dripped off her nose. He took the saddle off and started over. After the horse was saddled, he led it out.

She looked at the horse. "Dean will be mad because this is his favorite horse. Why he rode the other one today, I'll never know, but I can't worry about that now."

"Grandpa will handle Dean. Don't worry about him." He helped her mount up, and they rode out together. Killian's horse was about twelve inches higher than the one Alberta was on.

As they left the street, they turned down the main road through the town. As they were riding along, Killian saw Molly come out of the store. He smiled, and she did a double take and laughed because that seemed to be the only place he ever saw her. He tipped his hat, and she did a small curtsy.

Alberta looked over at him. "You know Molly McGuire?"

"Yeah, we have become acquainted."

"She's a nice girl. Are you sweet on her?"

"I don't know. I like to be with her and talk to her. I'm thinking about going back to school and finishing the eleventh and twelfth grades. She said she'd teach me."

Alberta looked back. "Not many men would do that, but you're not the average man." She smiled.

He smiled back.

They rode on, and at noon, Killian pulled two sandwiches out and handed one to Alberta. "Do you want to stop and eat?"

She shook her head. "If it's all right with you, I'd rather keep riding."

"It is. Here, have some water."

She took the canteen, drank, and handed it back to him.

"I heard it was bad between you and Uncle Dean. What can you do to make it better?"

"Do you know about—?"

"About your quilting class? Yeah, I know. What was your attraction to that guy?"

She was quiet for a few minutes. Killian looked at Alberta. She was a handsome woman, and even though she had had several kids, she had a good figure. Her brown hair had a slight natural curl and dropped to her shoulders.

She looked at Killian. "I happen to run into him at the market. He courted me years ago, before I met Dean. It's just that—" She stopped talking.

Killian looked over at her. "He made you feel like Dean did when you first met?"

She turned quickly. "Exactly. He made me feel like I was the most special person in the world. Dean has changed so much since we married. He's always unhappy about everything. He's really unhappy about Thomas taking a special interest in you." There was another long pause. "I just want you to know that when I went to his house, he was a gentleman. I mean we…we…kissed, but I never got in bed with him." There was another long pause. "It would have happened though, eventually. I'm not trying to make excuses for my actions."

Killian thought for a moment. "We know what you did was wrong, but Dean has to take some responsibility for this too."

She quickly interjected, "Why? He didn't do anything."

"He didn't do anything, including make you feel special, show that he loves you, and tell you how much he needs you. Did he do any of that?"

She shook her head. "Thanks. I don't feel as bad about myself as I did before."

"Maybe you should try to see it from the other standpoint and make him feel special. Have you tried that?"

"I really have. I knew he was mad at me and still is. I don't know what else I can do."

"When the time comes, you need to be ready to tell him you still love him, if you still do, and tell him you are ready to meet him halfway. If he agrees to try to save the marriage and will treat you as he's supposed to, then you'll be the wife that you're supposed to be. His inattention to you is what started this whole thing. I lay this at his doorstep."

Alberta rode silently for a while with tears in her eyes again. "I'm glad you came on this trip. You certainly have the gift of wisdom."

"Grandpa says I do, but I still doubt that."

"No, no. What you say is true, and anybody should be able to see that…except an eighteen-year-old unmarried boy. I'm surprised you can see past Molly McGuire."

He smiled. "Sometimes, I can't. I think about her an awful lot."

She adjusted her reins. "I would think you're in love with her, but boys your age don't know love from lust. So go slow, is all the advice I can give you."

He cleared his throat. "Sound advice it is, too." They both rode along silently, thinking about the important people in their lives.

Killian was often surprised by how he could look at things, such as Alberta and Dean's marriage, and see the problem and the solution. He attributed this to being the seventh son, but it always amazed him.

Just before sundown, they came to a small town, and Killian asked if there was a boardinghouse. A man pointed them in the right direction, and they stopped. Killian walked up to the boardinghouse and knocked on the door. It was an old house but seemed to be well maintained. A woman opened the door, and he asked if she might have two rooms for his aunt and him. She nodded, and he walked back out, took the saddlebags and Alberta's satchel, and carried them into the house. The woman pointed them to two rooms that were next to each other. "That will be a dollar for the two of you, and supper will be ready in an hour."

Killian paid her and then went back out to take the horses around to the back. He took their bridles off and let them graze for a while. Then he took them to a lean-to and took their saddles off.

Killian went back in as the woman was serving dinner, but Alberta was not there. He walked to her room and knocked several times. Finally, she came to the door and apologized for falling asleep. They ate dinner and then they both went back to their rooms and went to sleep. Alberta was obviously unwinding from the stress that had robbed her of sleep for the past few years.

Killian was up at dawn. He went out and saddled the horses before breakfast and then went to Alberta's room and knocked. She came to the door obviously just waking up. She apologized and got dressed and came out with her satchel. Killian set it by the door and took her into the dining room. After they had eaten, he tied her satchel on her horse, and she came out and he helped her up. They started down the road again.

122

Killian looked over at her. "You must be tired to sleep that much and that hard."

Alberta didn't smile. "To tell you the truth, I haven't slept very well since Dean and I started having our troubles, which has been for about three years. I guess your understanding me has taken a load off my shoulders, and I thank you for that."

They rode all day, eating lunch in the saddle again. Late in the afternoon, Alberta stopped. "There's nothing between here and the house. Dean and I slept in the woods up ahead. Tomorrow we can go cross-country and cut off about fifteen miles." After a few more hours of riding, Alberta pointed. "In these woods to the right is where we slept before."

They walked the horses in and found a shady spot by a small creek. Killian unsaddled the horses and tied them to a tree. He started a fire and sat back. They ate another sandwich out of Gretchen's supply. They were talking about the family when they heard a voice say, "Well, well. What do we have here?"

Killian got up, and there stood two huge men, who were obviously brothers. They had big, long, black beards and wore worn overalls and brogans. One of them looked at the other one and said, "Go take care of the kid, and I will talk to the little lady."

Alberta ran around a tree screaming. She and the first man were circling the tree like two kids. Killian saw that the other man was walking with a bad limp. Killian noted that it was his left knee, just like Dean's. As the man reached out to grab him, Killian ducked and kicked him in the knee with all he had. The man screamed and hit the ground hard. It was obvious that the leg was broken. Alberta was screaming so loudly that the man who was pursuing her didn't hear his brother. Or maybe he thought it was Killian because he didn't turn around.

Killian picked up a limb he had brought for the fire and swung it with all his might at the back of the man's head as he ran around the tree after Alberta. There was a loud crack, and Killian didn't know if it was the limb or the man's head. The man went to his knees and felt his head with his hand. Killian took what was left of the limb and brought it down over the top of the man's head, smashing his hand.

The man brought his hand down, and Killian hit him in the side of his head. He fell over and didn't move.

Killian saw that the man was wearing a gun. He reached down and pulled it out of his holster. He then turned to the other man. When the man saw him coming, he reached for his own gun, but Killian pointed the gun at his head.

"I wouldn't." Killian said with a determined look on his face, and the man knew he would shoot.

He went over and pulled the man's gun out. He made the man sit up against a tree. He took the bridle off one of the mules the two men were riding. He unsaddled the animal and slapped it with the reins, and it took off. He did the same with the other mule. He brought the bridles over and with his pocketknife, he cut the reins off the bit. He said to the man sitting at the tree, "Put your hands behind your back."

The man looked over his shoulder. "I can't. My knee's paining me too bad.

Killian slapped the reins around the tree and they whipped across the man's face. He put his hands behind him. Killian tied the man's hands tightly and then tied them to the tree. The man winced. "You got the blood cut off. I can't feel my hands."

"You won't need hands anyway after the wolves get through with you."

The man searched the woods for any sign of a wolf.

"Wolves haven't been seen around here for years."

Killian checked the ties. "Well, there's at least one, according to the tracks over here in the creek. It'll be interesting to see if he comes after you or your brother first."

Killian walked over and tied the unconscious man's hands, but he wasn't near a tree and the man was too big to move. Killian pulled the man's legs up and tied his hands to his feet. The other man was watching with great interest. "You're not going to leave us here to die, are you?"

"That's exactly what I'm going to do. You obviously meant us harm, so I'm going to return it tenfold."

It was dark by then, so Killian looked at Alberta. "Get some sleep. I'll stay up and watch. I don't think they can get undone, but I'm not going to take the chance."

Alberta lay down, and the man started yelling, "Help! Help!"

Killian walked over to him. He took the man's gun, cocked it, and placed the barrel on his good knee.

The man had a look of panic. "No, please no. I'll be quiet."

Killian uncocked the gun and sat down. Alberta got up, came over, and lay down beside him.

Killian sat leaning up against a log. When he got sleepy, he would get up and add firewood from the stack he had made or walk around. He sat back down about midnight, and Alberta sat up.

"Get some sleep," she said. "I'll watch for a while."

He handed her a gun, and she shook her head.

"I'll wake you up, and you can shoot it."

He smiled and lay down on his bedroll. It wasn't cold, but he felt a little cool, so he covered up.

Killian woke up knowing that something was wrong. Alberta had lain down next to him, gotten under the blanket, and was sound asleep. Killian raised his head and looked at both men. The one tied to a tree looked as if he had been struggling, but he was still tied, and he was asleep. The other one didn't look as if he had moved.

Killian shook Alberta, and she jumped awake. "I'm sorry. I was a little cold, so I thought I could cover up and stay awake."

"No harm done. Let's get packed up and get out of here."

He got up and saddled the horses, brought them over, and then tied on the saddlebags and bedroll. He did Alberta's also.

As they got on, the man tied to the tree woke up. "You're not going to leave us like this, are you? What if there's wolves around? That'll be murder."

"I doubt they could pin murder on a wolf. When I get to the next town, I'll tell somebody where you are. Good luck with the wolf," he said as they rode away.

When they got to the road, Alberta asked, "Do you really think a wolf will get them?"

Killian smiled. "I didn't see any wolf tracks. I was just trying to put a scare into them."

She started laughing. "I didn't know I was supposed to stay up and watch them. I was looking for wolves." She laughed again. Killian laughed too.

They rode on, and she pointed across a field. "That way. We should be at my mom's house before dark."

They rode hard and met a man coming down the road. He had a badge on, and Killian spoke to Alberta in a low voice. "Let me do the talking." As they drew closer, Killian raised his hand to show there was nothing in it. "Howdy, officer," he said.

The man touched the brim of his hat. "My name is Marshal John Harball, and I'm looking for two no-goods. They molested a woman and robbed a dry goods store back down the road a ways. Have you seen two big guys with black beards riding a couple of mules?"

Killian looked behind him. "Yes, sir. We were camped last night in the woods, and they came in and tried to get me and my aunt. I kicked one in his bad knee and laid the other one out with a club while he was chasing my aunt. He hasn't moved, and I fear he may be dead. It wasn't my intention to kill him."

"No matter. It will save me from hanging him if he is dead. Now where did you leave them?"

"Well, it's hard to describe because we came across country, but if you go down this road and turn left on the Knoxville road, you'll come to a little creek crossing the road. They are by the creek to your left. The brush is kind of dense right there, but if you go up another two hundred feet, you can get in there real easy."

"Much obliged." The marshal rode off.

Alberta looked concerned. "Do you really think that man is dead?"

"I don't know. I hit him in the head three times, and he hasn't moved a muscle since. Don't worry about it. We did all we could do."

Alberta rode on silently for a while. "What if you find out he was dead? Will that bother you?"

"I suppose it will to some extent, but what bothers me is the fact that he could have killed me, and I won't mention what they would've done to you."

"I see what you mean. If you hadn't, it might have been a lot worse for us. I know you didn't mean to kill him."

They rode on for the rest of the day. About midafternoon, Alberta pointed. "Turn up this road," she said.

They rode on for another hundred yards, and there was a house built on the side of a hill. There were several horses and buggies as well as saddle horses there.

Alberta bit her lower lip. "Oh Lord, I hope she hasn't died."

She jumped down, and Killian took her reins. He walked the horses over to a creek across the road and watered them, and then he tied them to a tree. He walked up a hill that led to one end of the porch. The other end of the porch was about fifteen feet off the ground because of the hill. He asked a man standing there if there was a well or a spring. The man pointed out the well, and Killian took his canteen over, pulled up a bucket of water, and filled it. He carried it back and hung on his saddle. He then walked up on the porch and spoke to the men sitting there. They were all bearded and wore overalls, and some were barefoot. They all wore old hats, pulled down over their foreheads. Most of them were missing at least some teeth.

They nodded an acknowledgment to Killian. One man, about thirty, sneered at him, saying, "It's bad enough our sister had to marry an Irishman. Why did she have to bring one down here with her?"

The man sitting in a chair looked up. "Let it go, Jeremy. You're not solving anything."

Jeremy stood up. "I could solve something if I knocked him on his ass, couldn't I?" He looked at Killian and walked down to the end of the porch. "What about it, boy? You want to fight me?" He looked back at the other men.

"OK," Killian said. He slugged Jeremy, knocking him off the end of the porch. Jeremy fell the fifteen feet and landed in the leaves, unconscious. Killian looked at the other men.

One man, who was standing in the yard, walked up the porch steps. "Are we going to let him get away with hitting Jeremy?" he asked.

The man in the chair turned to him. "If you want to get your ass whipped too, go on down there and take a swing at that fighting Irishman."

The man walked toward Killian, and when he got about three feet from him, Killian heard a thud, and the man fell to the floor. That's when he saw Alberta standing there with a rolling pin.

Another man said, "Bertie, you could have killed David hitting him with that rolling pin."

Alberta turned to him. "I still may kill him and anybody else who messes with this boy. There were three women murdered around us, and he was sent down here for my protection. Now leave him alone or deal with me."

She looked at Killian. "Killian, come inside. I want you to see Momma." She took him into a room that was very primitive. It had tattered curtains, and Killian could see chickens underneath the house through the floorboards. There was a woman lying there who looked dead. Alberta touched her hand.

"Momma, I want you to meet my nephew, Killian."

The woman's weak eyes opened wide, and she reached out her hand toward Killian and grabbed his hand.

She smiled, and in a low raspy voice, said, "Killian, the seventh son of the seventh son." She dropped her hand, and her eyes were fixed.

Alberta started weeping. "She's dead. Good-bye, Momma." Tears were flowing.

Killian helped Alberta up and closed the old woman's eyes. He walked out on the porch with her, and she announced that their mother was dead. Even the men started crying.

Killian took up his place on the end of the porch. One of the men who had been standing inside came over to him. "I'm Uncle Harold. She was my sister. What was it she said when she reached for your hand? I couldn't hear."

Killian shook his head. "I couldn't either."

The man said he would go ask Bertie and left.

Alberta came out of the house, saying, "I don't know what she said, Uncle Harold. I didn't hear it."

She walked over to Killian. He put his arm around her, and she leaned on him and cried.

Everybody got in line to view the old woman one last time, but Killian stayed on the porch, holding his hand.

Alberta came back out and saw him. "What's wrong with your hand?" she asked. She picked it up and saw that the skin was burned. She could see where her mother had grabbed it. She looked back to make sure no one could hear her. "How did that happen?"

Killian shook his head. "I don't know."

"But how did she know about you?"

Killian shook his head again. "I don't know. I don't understand it myself."

Alberta smiled a weak smile. "Whatever happened, it made her happy. I'm thankful for that. She'll be buried in the family cemetery out back, and we can start back in the morning."

"Whenever you're ready. We can stay as long as you want."

She shook her head. "No, if I stay, I may have to kill one of my brothers."

Killian walked off the porch and around to the back of the house. He saw the family cemetery. A grave had been started. The shovel was sticking up in the dirt, so Killian picked it up and started digging. He stepped on the shovel, pushing it deep into the earth. He dug a hole about six feet deep, and eight feet in length.

"Let me have a go at it." It was the man who had been sitting on the porch. He offered Killian his hand, and Killian grabbed it and pulled himself out. A couple of men carried a crude casket out of the barn and took it into the house. Killian took another turn at digging and finished the grave.

The minister had arrived, and they were ready to start the service. Killian stood way back, out of the way. After it was over, Alberta came over to him. "They told me you dug the grave. Thank you for that."

Killian smiled. "I helped dig it. There were others."

About that time, Uncle Harold walked up with tears in his eyes. "My time ain't too far off. I have to know what she said. One of you must have heard it."

He paused, and then said, "It sounded like she said something about the seventh son. Are you the seventh son of a seventh son? Some folks say that a seventh son of a seventh son is coming, and he'll be named Killian. Isn't that your name?"

Alberta looked at Killian, not knowing how to answer. Killian looked at the old man. "Maybe she remarked that I had the same name as the seventh son, but I only have four brothers."

Uncle Harold looked at Killian as if he didn't believe him. "Will you promise me one thing? Will you be at my funeral?"

Killian nodded. "Yes, sir, I will make you that promise, but I hope you have a long, happy life."

Uncle Harold nodded. "That's not likely, but when I get ready to go, I'm going to wait on you like she did." He walked off crying.

The next morning, Alberta was up early and packed some food from all the dishes that had been brought over by family and friends. Killian packed it in the saddlebag and put his bedroll on his horse. He had slept on the floor in front of the fireplace. Killian went out and mounted his horse, which was on the other side of the road. He sat there and waited for Alberta as she bade farewell to her friends and family. She finally started over, and Killian met her with her horse.

The trip back was uneventful. They picked a different place to sleep that first night and slept at the same boardinghouse the second night. They pulled onto the street where they lived about three o'clock, and Killian saw Grandpa sitting on the front porch. He took care of Alberta's horse and put it away, and then rode home.

Thomas looked at him as he walked up the steps. "Anything eventful happen?'

Killian told him about the two men and that he thought he had killed one of them. He told him about knocking one of Alberta's brothers off the porch, and Alberta cracking another one in the head with a rolling pin. He told him about the talk they'd had about her relationship with Dean. The last thing he told Thomas was about the old woman knowing who he was, and he showed him his hand. Thomas looked at it. "Better put some butter on that."

"It's not a heat burn. It doesn't hurt, and it's already going away."

Thomas didn't understand it either. Killian leaned down and opened the saddlebags, and he pulled out the two guns and handed them to Thomas.

Thomas took the guns and stood up. "Why don't you go put your horse up and come back and sit?" he said.

"Grandpa, I'm going to ride up to the store. I'll be back."

Thomas looked at him suspiciously. "What do you need from the store?"

"Nothing." Killian smiled as he mounted up and rode off. He stopped at the store and saw that Molly wasn't in there, so he rode down toward the park. He saw her sitting on a swing, reading a book. He got off his horse, tied it up at a hitching post, and walked up behind her. "Need a push, little girl?"

She recognized his voice. "I suppose so."

She handed him her book. He laid it on the ground nearby and gave her a push. She swung up and back. He wasn't pushing her hard, but he loved touching her when he did.

134

Over her shoulder, she asked, "Where have you been? I haven't seen you all week."

"My Aunt Alberta's mother died in Seymour, and I had to ride down there with her for the funeral."

"That was awfully nice of you. It's dangerous for a woman out alone."

They talked until the sun started going down.

She stopped the swing. "Well, I must get home before dark. When were you going to call on me? You said you would."

"How about tomorrow night, about six? Are you and your family finished eating by then? I can wait until later, if need be."

"That's about the time we get through, so why don't you come about five and eat with us?"

"Don't you think you ought to check with your parents first?"

"No. Five it is, then."

"Would I be too forward offering you a ride on the back of my horse? Or I will let you ride and I will walk you to your house."

She smiled. "It would be too forward tonight, but not tomorrow night." She smiled and quickly walked off.

Killian went back home, sat in his rocker, and listened to it creak as he told Thomas what he had done.

Thomas rocked. "I don't see any harm in that, unless you get serious about this girl."

"What would be the harm in that?"

"You're just eighteen. You should experience several girlfriends before you get serious enough to marry her. How does her father feel about his eighteen-year-old daughter liking someone?"

Killian looked at Thomas. "She's twenty years old, so it must not be an issue."

"She's twenty? You don't mind her being older than you? I knew she taught school, but I didn't figure her being twenty years old."

"It's not uncommon for a man to be that much older—or more—than his wife. What does it matter if the age difference is the other way around?"

Thomas shook his head but said nothing.

Chapter 10

The next day, Killian and Thomas rode out to the gristmill. They were grinding corn into meal. Uncle Jeffery walked over to them. "Old man Farber's giving me a hard time," he said.

Thomas looked at Jeffery. "Over what?"

"Oh, he brought his corn in before Wallace did, but I ground Wallace's first."

Killian didn't look at Jeffery. "Why?"

Jeffery looked at him. "Why don't you go away while I talk to my father, little boy."

Thomas gave Jeffery a look. "Don't talk that way to him. Answer his question."

"All right. I did Wallace's first because he's a bigger client than Farber. I don't want to make him mad at us. Does that answer your question?"

Killian stared at him. "What will happen if you do it on a first-come, first-serve basis?"

"We may lose his business."

Killian looked back at the mill. "Where's he going to take it? Where is the closest gristmill?"

Thomas looked at Jeffery. "About eighty miles south."

"Then there's not a threat of losing his business. Treat Farber fair next time and do all business on a first-come, first-serve basis."

Jeffery jumped down off the porch. "Who are you to give me orders about my gristmill?"

Killian had taken a step forward to hit him, but Thomas stepped in. "Jeffery, it's not your gristmill; it's mine. Do what he says and do it on a first-come basis. Do you hear me?"

Jeffery was seething, but he nodded. "Yes, sir."

Killian asked Thomas, "Which one is Farber?"

Thomas pointed. "The one in the red shirt over there."

Killian walked over and introduced himself to Bob Farber. "I want to apologize for your treatment. My grandfather has instructed my uncle Jeffery to grind corn on a first-come basis from now on. If he doesn't, please come see my grandfather...or me."

Mr. Farber shook Killian's hand. "I appreciate that. Why doesn't your grandfather let you run this business and put that asshole somewhere else?"

"Maybe he will one day. Maybe he will." He walked away.

They got on their horses and left.

Thomas was proud that Killian would take charge in any given situation. He admired that willingness, but he was afraid at the same time. He didn't know if anyone in town was smart enough to see that Killian's maturity had to come from some source.

Thomas talked to Killian as they rode home. "You need to work on your dealing with other people. Sometimes if you ask, you get better cooperation."

"Do you think Uncle Jeffery would have changed his ways if I had asked politely?"

"No, I don't. But still, try it in certain situations."

Killian nodded. They rode up past the ironworks, and Killian and Thomas noticed that the windows were open. They kept going.

As they made it up to the mountain road, Killian asked, "Do you know where the McGuires live?"

Thomas smiled. "I'll show you on the way."

When they got to the main road, they turned toward town, and before they got to the park, Thomas pointed to his right. "Down there, on your right, there's a yellow house with a steep roof. You can't miss it. That's the McGuire house."

That evening at four thirty, Killian started down the road. He had on his best suit and polished shoes. He didn't have a hat without a sweat ring on it, so he didn't wear one. He walked his horse right up to the hitching rail in front of the house.

Molly came out when she heard him. "You're right on time. Come in and let me introduce you to the family."

"Actually, I'm a little early. I didn't know how long it would take to get here."

"You're not early." They walked into the house, and Molly took him over to her parents. "Killian, this is my mother and this is my father, Mildred and John McGuire. Mother and Father, this is Killian O'Rourke."

John was a fit-looking man about five feet seven inches. He had medium-brown hair and a moustache. He looked pressed and clean. Molly's mother was an inch taller than John was. She had reddish-brown hair, but not the fiery-red hair that he and Molly had. She was well dressed and had her hair piled on her head, as was the style for women of her stature.

Killian bowed his head slightly. "Pleased to make your acquaintance, Mr. and Mrs. McGuire. I appreciate the invitation for dinner."

Molly showed him where to sit, and Mr. McGuire looked at him. "So you're that O'Rourke. You came in and made the old man raise the windows. I was in the last row. We all appreciate what you did."

Killian shrugged and said, "It was the right thing to do. My uncle Patrick didn't know he was keeping the windows closed in this heat, or he would have changed it himself."

"Well, what are you going to be doing for your grandfather?"

"My grandfather is showing me around and trying to find the place that I might best fit."

A man walked in the door about that time, and John stood up. "This is my brother, Eldridge. He works for the woolen mill across town. Eldridge, this is Killian O'Rourke, recently from Ireland."

Eldridge looked like John, but he was very thin compared with John. He had the same hair and moustache.

Eldridge came over and shook his hand. "What a coincidence. I'm leaving for Ireland in two days. Where did you live, Killian?"

"Outside of Queenstown on the southern coast. My father and brothers have a small farm."

Eldridge looked surprised. "Well, isn't it a small world. That's exactly where I am going. Does your family have sheep?"

"Yes, sir, about two hundred."

"Then I'm sure I'll be seeing your mother and father. What's their name? Oh, of course, O'Rourke. I don't know what I was thinking. Do you have other family there?"

"Just my father and…four brothers. My ma died a year ago."

Eldridge nodded. "Oh, I'm sorry, but if I see you father and brothers, I will be sure to say hello for you."

"I would appreciate that very much."

Eldridge looked at Molly's mother and back at Killian. "I have my own place down a ways, but I come in here for Mildred's cooking as often as she and John will have me."

Mildred looked disappointed at him. "You have been told you're always welcome and need no invitation. Now, let's go into the dining room. Dinner's ready."

Killian had never had such a meal. He had pork chops again, with potatoes, but they were like a pudding. They had been mashed and stirred, and he could see the swirls of butter in them. They were simply delicious.

Molly looked at Killian and smiled. "Killian said he had to fight his brothers for a place at the table back home." She laughed.

Mildred looked over at him and said, "With four brothers, I bet you did, didn't you."

Killian smiled as he looked down. "I may have been exaggerating a bit. My brothers and I fought a lot, but not at the table. We would have had to fight my father if we'd done that."

They all laughed.

"Are you finished with school, Killian?"

Molly turned her head to her mother. "Mother, that's not a question to ask someone."

Mildred looked surprised. "Oh, I'm so sorry."

Killian answered anyway. "It's no problem. I don't mind. As a matter of fact, I finished the tenth grade, and Molly said she would help me complete the two remaining ones."

They all turned toward Molly, and her mother said, "Oh really? How nice. If you finished…how old are you, if I may ask?"

Killian felt as if maybe he had said too much, but he couldn't back out now, so he said, "Eighteen, but I'll be nineteen soon."

Mildred raised her eyebrows. "Oh really? I have a birthday soon too. When is yours?"

142

Killian smiled. "In less than eight months."

Everybody laughed, but Mildred didn't laugh as hard as the others did, and she cut her eyes at Molly.

After they finished eating, Molly took Killian by the hand. "Killian, let's go sit on the porch. Father, will you light a lamp for us?"

John stood up. "Of course. I'll light the one by the door, and you can sit on the swing and maybe the bugs won't bother you."

When Killian got to the swing, he asked Molly, "Did I go too far in telling them how old I was?"

"No, the truth is never the wrong answer." She smiled.

Killian looked at her for a minute. "I saw the look your mother gave you. She was surprised that I was younger than you, wasn't she?"

"Don't look into my eyes like that. There's something mysterious in your soul, but I can't tell what it is."

"OK, but you're trying to change the subject."

Molly sighed. "OK. I might as well tell you. My mother has my life planned out to the last detail. I am to marry a man four years older than myself. He has to be a professional man or a musician. She has picked out such a man for me, and I won't give him the time of day."

"Well, that leaves me out of the running. I'm neither. This guy is not the guy I slugged at the park, is it?"

"No. David is a bully that my parents have told me to stay away from. The guy they want me to start seeing is a clerk at the bank. His father owns it and has his life planned for him too. But he has his eye on a girl who dresses…well, let's say, less than ladylike."

Killian picked up her hand and held it. "What are your plans for yourself?"

"Well, I want to love the man I marry; that's a must. My parents think that I'm wasting my life because I am unmarried at twenty. I may be thirty before I find the right man."

"Well, you like me, don't you?"

"You're very nice, but I don't think we'll be anything more than friends."

Killian could feel the pins in his hand from the lie she just told.

"So you don't think we couldn't become closer and marry someday?"

She looked wide-eyed. "I can't even think about marrying you." She paused. "I think we are incompatible in our characters."

Killian could feel the pins in his hand. He smiled.

She looked at him, trying not to smile. "Whatever are you smiling about?" she asked.

He lowered his voice. "You. You're actually cute when you lie."

"What lie have I told you? I must know."

"You're attracted to me in a strong way, just as I'm attracted to you. If we let this relationship take its normal course, we should be married in about a year."

She sat there with her mouth open. "I've never heard of such nerve." She stood up. "I think you should leave, and for your information, I'm not attracted to you in the—"

Killian stood her up and kissed her.

When he pulled away, he stayed close to her face and looked into her green eyes. "OK. If that's the way you feel, then I'll leave, never to darken your doorway again. You have my promise on that. Good night, Miss McGuire. Oh, and give my regards to your parents." He walked out to his horse, got on, and trotted off without looking back.

She stood there, stunned by the boldness of his kiss, and watched him ride away. She wanted to call out to him but knew she shouldn't. She wanted him to kiss her again—under her protest, of course.

He rode home, put his horse in Patrick's barn, and walked over to the house. As he approached the dark porch, he heard his grandfather say, "Well, how did it go?"

He sat down and decided to be forthcoming with his closest friend. "It didn't go well, I think. She told me she wasn't interested in me as a suitor. I told her she was lying and that we should be married in a year. I kissed her and left."

Thomas smiled. "You did right. Now she has to figure out how to right her wrong. You have her on the defensive."

Killian looked over at Thomas. "I can see trouble ahead."

"Another vision?"

"No, sir. I met her uncle, who is a wool buyer. He is leaving soon to go to Queenstown. He said he would look up my father and four brothers."

Thomas leaned forward. "Damn, I can't let you out of my sight. I'll have to think on this some."

The next morning, Killian was sitting on the porch when Thomas came out. Thomas sat down and said, "You're up early, aren't you? Gretchen said you already ate."

Killian nodded. "I've been thinking. Maybe I need to go to work with Patrick for a while, maybe weeks or months."

"Why? Do you want his job?"

"No, sir, but I need to know how everything works. Not only at the ironworks, but also at the gristmill and the market. I don't mind starting at the bottom and working my way up, but I need to know what the overall product is supposed to be and what it should cost to make it and how much it's supposed to sell for."

Thomas looked back. "What about school? You can't spend the day with Paddy and go to school too."

Killian thought for a minute. "I'll have to think on that some."

Thomas was quietly proud because Killian was sounding more like him every day.

"In the meantime, go down and be Paddy's shadow for a couple of days. I'm going to tell him to stay with you every minute."

The next morning, Patrick rode over. "You going with me today?" he asked Killian. "If so, let's go."

Killian got up and started for his horse, wondering when Thomas had had a talk with Patrick. As they rode together, neither one said anything until Patrick looked over at him. "Be truthful with me. Is Papa setting you up to take my job?"

Killian smiled. "No, he's not. First, I wouldn't have your job if it was offered to me, and it won't be. Grandfather wants me to learn business in general, and he figures you're the best to teach me."

"Fair enough, but I think you ought to start working in the foundry and work your way up. Learn every job by doing it."

"That's what I told him. He wants you to teach me the business overall, and after I get through going through the gristmill and the market, maybe he'll put me somewhere I can do that."

Patrick frowned. "Did you really tell him you wanted to work your way up?"

Killian nodded. When they got to the ironworks, Killian followed Patrick around, seeing how things worked and sitting in on meetings. The employees eyed him cautiously, wondering if he was being trained to take one of their jobs.

At noon, Patrick asked, "Did you bring lunch?"

Killian shook his head.

Patrick looked up the hill. "There's a little store up on the main road. You can get something there, but bringing it will be cheaper. Try to be back in an hour."

Killian almost ran to his horse. He didn't want to waste any time if he happened to run into Molly. He dismounted in front of the store and went in. Off to the side were tables and chairs where people could sit and eat. Killian got a plate of vegetables and a piece of bread. He got some coffee and sat down at an empty table. He looked around and saw Molly sitting at a table eating with a man. He pretended he didn't see her. A few seconds later, she was standing at his table with a plate of food. "May I join you?"

"Only if you don't pick a fight. We're just friends, you understand."

She looked embarrassed. "Don't tease me. I feel bad enough about how I treated you. I want to apologize."

"Sure, have a seat." He stood up as she sat down.

She clasped her hands and looked at him. "I apologize for my actions last night."

"What actions are you talking about? Just to be clear."

"My telling you to leave. I didn't really want you to. I don't know why I said that. I think it was because you were so bold in the way you talked. We shouldn't be talking of love and marriage."

Killian looked at her. "You said it was never wrong to speak the truth. Should I deny my feelings like you're doing? Doesn't seem healthy to me. Do you think I should apologize for kissing you? Sorry, I can't do

148

that, because I enjoyed it too much and will do it again, given the chance. So where does that leave us?"

Molly looked down. "I guess I do deny my feelings. It's just that it was so bold. I'm not used to a man talking to me in such a way." She looked at him and then lowered her eyes. "I did enjoy the kiss too. I've never had anybody kiss me like that."

"Twenty years old and never been kissed? I find that hard to believe," Killian said with a smile.

"For your information, I didn't say I have never been kissed. I said I have never been kissed like that." She looked into Killian's stare. "Don't look at me like that. What mysterious secret are you hiding? I can see it in your eyes."

Killian looked away. "I do have a secret, but I can't tell you. It's something that you will have to discover yourself. Now, the best way is to kiss me as often as you can. That will reveal the secret, I'm sure."

She blushed. "That's not true. You're teasing me again."

"Yes, I am, and I must go back to work. I don't want to be late the first day on the job, do I?"

She looked surprised. "Work? I thought you were going to school."

"That's something we need to get together and talk about. I'll be riding past the park about 5:15 today. I might sit at a picnic table and think about that. Good day to you, Molly McGuire."

He paid for his lunch and walked out. He got back to the ironworks and was barely on time.

Patrick looked up as he walked in. "That must have been one hell of a lunch."

Killian smiled. "I ran into an old friend."

"Molly McGuire, I presume. You two would make a good couple, except there's no way your children wouldn't be redheaded."

Killian laughed.

Patrick leaned back. "There aren't any redheads in the family other than you and father."

Killian looked surprised, and Patrick nodded. "Oh, he is gray-headed now, but he had the same red hair as you in his younger days. Have any of your brothers got red hair?"

Killian shook his head. "Only my father."

"Father has red hair, and then his seventh son has red hair, and *his* seventh son has red hair. There's a lot more to that than coincidence, I suppose."

Killian followed Patrick all day and mostly listened, making mental notes about things he wanted to ask Thomas about. They were in and out of meetings. They walked the ironworks floor several times. It was a clean place, despite the molten material and the metal spurs flying as edges were ground. At five, Patrick and Killian walked out and rode off.

As they approached the park, Killian scanned the people and finally saw Molly. She was at the picnic table they'd shared before. "Excuse me, Uncle," he said. "I see a friend I want to talk to."

He tied his horse to a hitching post. Before he reached Molly, another man sat down and started talking to her. But Killian wasn't going to let that deter him. He removed his hat, took a deep breath and he slowly, but deliberately walked over to the table.

"Am I late?"

She looked up. "No, you're right on time."

Killian sat down by her. "Now where were we? Oh yeah, you just said you had never been—"

"Excuse us, will you, Johnny? This is rather personal," Molly pleaded.

Johnny gave Killian a dirty look, but he got up and walked away.

She turned her head to him. "You weren't really going to talk about kissing in front of him, were you?"

Killian laughed. "No, but I needed to be alone with you and figured you would get rid of him. What do you want to talk about other than having never been kissed like I kissed you?"

She tried to look as if she was mad, but a smile ruined it. "Let's talk about your going to school. How are you going to work and go to school too?"

"Well, do you teach after regular school hours? I could stop by your house, after I got off from work, but that would monopolize your time, and Johnny or your banker would probably not like that."

"I don't care what either of them likes. Johnny has a sweetheart, so I don't know why he even stopped to talk to me, and I told you the other guy has his eye on a…another woman."

Killian added, "Who dresses less than ladylike."

She smiled. "Yes. I knew you'd remember that part. But what you said about after school hours? You could come by my house, and I could give you lessons. Since you are my only student, you could take as long as you needed to complete the lessons."

"Talk to your parents and tell me what they say—and don't tell me you don't have to talk to them. After that look your mother gave you, you need to check with her, at least. Let me know before we decide to do anything."

"It's not that Mother doesn't like you. It's just that—"

"I'm not four years older than you or a professional man or a musician."

"Those are my mother's standards, but they're not mine. She'll have to learn sooner or later that I am my own woman."

"What's taking her so long? I suspected that when I first met you and fully realized it after I kissed you."

"You're teasing me again. I must go. I'm already late for dinner."

"Let me give you a ride home. You said it would be OK after the other night."

She smiled. "Maybe."

They walked out to his horse, and he led it over to a mounting block.

She looked at the horse. "You have such a tall horse."

She climbed up and sat sidesaddle behind the saddle. He threw his leg over the saddle horn. She put her arms around him, and they rode off. When they got to her house, he slid down and held his hands out for her. She slid off the horse with his help, and when her lips were even with his, he kissed her again.

She looked shocked. "What if my father saw that?"

"He didn't. That's the reason I have a tall horse. I'll see you at lunch tomorrow?"

"No. I have to go somewhere with my mother."

He winked at her, mounted up, and rode off.

When he got home, Thomas was sitting on the porch. Killian looked at Thomas. "I'm sorry I didn't send word about being late."

Thomas smiled. "Paddy told me where you were. Is that going to be a ritual from now on?"

"It remains to be seen. She's going to talk to her parents about me coming over after work and her teaching me then. At least I won't be sitting at a desk too small for me with a bunch of children."

"Yes, but it's still going to take effort to work and complete your schoolwork too. What if you get behind on assignments?"

Killian thought for a minute. "Well, I was hoping she would keep me after school anyway." Thomas and Killian both laughed.

Thomas looked at him with approval. "Honestly, I want you to finish school. If we have to cut your hours short at work, we can do that."

That night about midnight, Killian had another vision. He could see a building burning way off in the distance. People were jumping out of windows and screaming. The vision seemed to last forever, and he finally woke himself up. He got up and started for Thomas's room, when he was drawn to the front door.

He looked out and up the street, and then off in the distance he saw an orange glow in the sky. He knew it was the building from his dream. He ran and woke Thomas up, and they went out on the porch, Thomas in his nightshirt and Killian in his underwear.

Thomas looked down the dark road toward the fire. The blaze was obviously many miles away. "Well, it's of no significance to us personally that we know of. The only thing that concerns me is your having the vision when it happened. Your other visions were a couple of days before and in one case, a week before. Let me know when you have another one, no matter how insignificant it may seem to you, OK?"

Killian nodded, and they went back to bed.

The next day, Killian was at the ironworks when Thomas came in. He motioned him to Patrick's office and shut the door. "The vision you saw last night was the old Chambers Hotel. Eighteen people died that they know of. What the significance of the vision is, I don't know."

Patrick looked at both of them. "You saw it before it happened?"

Thomas answered for him. "No, while it was happening." Then he looked at Killian and said, "I brought you lunch. You can't eat out every day on your pay. How much do we pay you?"

"Nothing. Why?"

"See? You can't eat out on that pay—can he, son?"

Patrick laughed and agreed.

Killian didn't mind; Molly had told him she wouldn't be able to meet him that day. She had to go somewhere with her mother. Killian thought that if that happened often, he would know it was Mrs. McGuire's design rather than coincidence.

He walked down a hall and out on the roof, where he had seen a table and chairs a few days before. He saw Dean sitting there and walked over. "May I join you?"

Dean looked up from his sandwich. "No. If you insist on staying, I'll leave."

He stared at Dean. "Why are you are so miserable? No one wants to be around you because you are the most miserable, negative person I've ever seen. Your own kids and dog avoid you, if you haven't noticed. Is it because of your family problems?"

Dean glared at him. "What in the hell would you know about my family problems?"

Killian sat down. "I know about your wife seeing that other man. In fact, she and I had a long talk about it, the six days I spent with her. Do you want to know what she said?"

Dean looked down. Then he looked back up and nodded.

"She said she realized what she did was wrong; she made no excuses about that. The most important thing she said was that she never got in bed with the man."

Dean smirked. "And you believe her?"

"She had no reason to lie to me. She knew I knew everything. She said they usually met at a restaurant or someplace like that, but one night, she went over to sleep with him—but she couldn't do it and she left. I asked her what attracted her to this man, and she said he was an old beau, and they had accidently met at the market. She said he treated her like she was royalty. He paid attention to her; he told her how pretty she was and made her feel like…what did she say it felt like? Oh yeah, she said he made her feel like you did when you first married her. Now Dean, there is no denying what she did was wrong, but you're going to have to take some blame for this."

"Why? I didn't do anything."

"That's right, you didn't. You didn't make her feel special, you didn't tell her how much you love her, you didn't pay attention to her and tell her that she's pretty. You didn't do your part to make the marriage work. Look, man, you're going to have to figure out if you want to stay married to this woman, and if you do, you have to try to save this marriage. If you don't, you are going to wake up someday, and she'll be gone with your kids. Do you want that?"

Dean's eyes filled with tears, and he shook his head.

Killian slapped the table. "Great. Now go home and ask her to forgive you. But stop on the way and get some flowers."

"I need to ask Patrick if I can leave. I'll be a minute."

"No, you don't. I'll tell him you had an emergency at home. Now go home while you still have a mind to."

Killian ate and went back in. Patrick was walking down the hall. "Where's Dean?"

"He had to go home for some family emergency. He probably won't be back today."

"Well, go home and find out what the emergency is. Tell him I need him back if he can get back."

"I know what kind of family emergency he has. We were talking about it, and he decided his marriage was worth saving and left. I don't know what the problem here is, but it's not more important than his problem."

"Well, you go down and figure out why we can't get more production out of the jobs room. They are putting out ten jobs a day, and we're losing money at that rate. I know they can do more."

"Let me see what I can do." He walked out.

Patrick stepped out of the office and added, "Don't fire or fight anybody."

Killian raised his hand in acknowledgment.

When he got to the jobs room, Killian went to the foreman. "I'm here to observe for my own education. Patrick said to see you because you know more than anyone here. What exactly is a job?"

The foreman, whose name was Burt, puffed out his chest. "Well, a job is getting raw materials in at the end of the building and doing everything we need to do to them—like tempering, blowing holes in a molten sheet, or cutting or bending it. It all depends on what we are making and for whom. Then we have to get the product out the other end of the building and shipped off. That's a job."

Killian nodded as if he was impressed. "How many jobs can you do in a shift?"

"About ten a day is about all we can handle."

"What's the record for number of jobs in a day?"

"Well, they did fourteen a few years back for a hurry-up order that had to be filled, but you can't do that day in and day out."

Killian nodded again. "One more question. Which shift produces the most jobs? I imagine the night shift or the graveyard shift would be the fastest."

Burt got red in the face. "Hell, neither one can hold a candle to this crew. This is the most productive shift."

Killian nodded again, thanked Burt, and walked off. When the whistle blew and the day shift walked out, Killian got a piece of the chalk they marked steel with and wrote on the concrete floor by the door, "Eleven jobs completed today by the day shift."

Before the night shift came in, he went upstairs. He looked down from the rail above and saw them looking at it.

At five o'clock, Killian and Patrick left. As they rode down the street, he saw Molly and her mother at the market. He rode on by without trying to attract her attention.

Patrick looked at him. "What's the problem? You don't like your mother-in-law?"

Killian cut his eyes at Patrick and smiled without saying anything.

Back home, he put his horse up, and as he walked over to the house, he spotted three kids playing in Thomas's peach orchard. Killian looked out at them and asked, "Are those Dean's kids? What are they doing here?"

Thomas looked across at the orchard. "I don't know what the hell is wrong with Dean. He come galloping in a little after noon with a handful of posies, ran in the house, and the next thing I know, his kids are here telling me that their momma told them to come over and play until she came for them. If she don't come soon, I'm going to take them back home."

Killian laughed. "You can remember back when you sent the kids off so you could be alone, don't you?"

Thomas narrowed his eyes at Killian.

Killian laughed again. "Hell, Papa would send all seven of us on a three-hour walk to Queenstown about once a month to get one damn block of cheese and eighteen biscuits. We wanted to tell him we knew what they were doing, which was fine with us, and we would be glad to sit out at the shearing shed for an hour or two, but no one was brave enough to tell him."

Thomas roared with laughter, and when he composed himself, he said, "I thought they were having problems."

"They are. Or rather, they were. They both saw their mistakes and are trying to make it work. I had a talk with Dean today. He's OK."

Thomas looked at Killian, amazed at his maturity. He was more and more proud of Killian and was grateful that he was the seventh son of the seventh son.

Gretchen called them in for dinner, and afterward they went back out on the porch and saw Dean and Alberta walking toward them. Alberta climbed the porch steps and took Killian's face in her hands. She kissed him on the mouth and smiled. Then she walked to the side of the porch and called, "Come on, kids! Let's go!"

As she thanked Thomas for watching them, Dean walked up and shook Killian's hand. "Thanks for everything." They walked home, herding their kids ahead of them.

The next morning, Killian went straight to the jobs room. There on the concrete was a sign on the floor in chalk. "Graveyard shift completed fourteen jobs today." He could see where the night shift had done twelve.

About that time, Burt came walking in and asked, "What the hell is this? All right, guys, listen up here. We're not going to let them bastards outdo us."

Killian walked away and went back to Patrick's office.

A few minutes later, Dean came in. "Paddy, that was ingenious getting the shifts to compete with each other."

Patrick asked, "What in the hell are you talking about?"

Dean looked at him with a questioning look. "You didn't write on the floor in chalk how many jobs each shift does? They're trying to outdo each other in the number of jobs they do, and they are already up to fourteen per shift."

Patrick looked back. "I didn't write anything in chalk." They both looked at Killian.

Killian smiled and said, "We should be doing at least sixteen jobs per shift, if not eighteen. Once we know they can handle it, we can require them to put that many out. Can't we? I mean, we don't want anybody getting hurt, but we can require them to complete a minimum number of jobs."

On the way home, Killian saw Molly and her mother riding toward him in a horse and cart. As they got near, Molly told her mother to stop, and she did, though reluctantly. Killian bid them both a good day.

Molly looked at him on his tall horse. "I haven't seen you much lately. Where have you been keeping yourself?"

Before he could answer, Mrs. McGuire picked up the reins and said, "We really must be going, Molly."

"Wait a minute, Mother, or let me out."

Her mother just sat there.

Killian looked down at her. "My routine hasn't changed. It's yours that's been taking up your time. If you don't want to see me, just say so." He smiled.

Molly looked hurt. "I didn't say I didn't want to see you. In fact, I do want to see you."

Killian glanced at her mother, who was looking in the other direction. "Well, somebody doesn't want us seeing each other, so when you figure that out, you know where I'll be. Good day." He tipped his hat and rode off.

Killian rode home, put his horse up, and walked over to the house, where Thomas was sitting on the front porch. Thomas asked about his day.

"Patrick and Dean have the jobs production up to fourteen a shift so far and will probably exceed that and then maintain it."

"Fourteen? Really? How in the hell did they do that?"

"Just sound management, best I can tell."

Thomas nudged him. "I think there's someone coming to see you."

Killian looked down the street and saw Molly coming in her cart, but she was alone. Thomas started to get up, but Killian put his hand on Thomas's hand. "Keep your seat," he said.

Killian got up and walked out into the street.

Molly waved at Thomas and said, "Good day, Mr. O'Rourke."

After Thomas acknowledged her greeting, she looked at Killian. "Get in. I need to talk to you."

Killian stepped over the edge of the cart and sat down across from her. She popped the whip over the horse's head, and they drove off.

Killian looked at her. "Just where are you taking me, and are your intentions honorable?"

She cut her eyes at him and smiled. She drove to the park, and they got out. They walked around, and she finally stopped and looked at him. "I realized what you meant when you looked at my mother. I was wondering why she was taking such an interest in me and wanting to take me places and buy me clothes. She was just trying to keep us apart. I intend to have a serious talk with her and Father when I get back."

"I wish I could be a fly on the wall for that one."

She frowned. "I'm serious. Mother is going to have to let up on me, or I'll find my own place to live."

They had walked to the middle of the park, and it was almost dark. Molly looked around and then tiptoed up and kissed Killian on the lips. It was just a peck—that was all she could reach. He smiled and put his hands under her arms, and he lifted her and kissed her full on the mouth. She put her arms around his neck, and the kiss seemed to last for five minutes.

He finally set her down and smiled. "Now, that's the way you're supposed to kiss. You should be kissed, kissed often, and by somebody who knows how."

She smiled as they started back. "You certainly know how. Where did you learn to kiss like that? Back in Ireland?"

"No, no. I just learned that myself. I'm as new at this as you are."

163

She laughed. "I don't believe you. I bet you got a girl back in Ireland just waiting for you to come back, don't you?"

He looked at her as seriously as he knew how. "No. I've never had a girl—in Ireland or anyplace else. I was too poor to have a girl, and the few eligible ones married my brothers."

Her eyes widened. "Really? You never had a sweetheart?"

He looked her in the eyes. "Only in my dreams, and it's always been you."

She kissed him again. "We have to go. I'll drive you home."

"Not after dark. Take me to your house, and I'll walk home. It's not that far."

She drove to her street and stopped. "I can see my house from here. Go on back, and I'm sorry to do this."

"After that kiss, I'll do it every night if you want to." He smiled. "What about school? Did your mother have a fit over it?"

"She didn't want me to, so I told her I was going to do it at our house or at yours. She decided our house would be best."

"You're smart. Maybe I can be smart like that someday."

"You're already that smart. What you will be is as educated as I am."

He kissed her quickly before anybody could come by, and he watched her drive to her house before he started walking home. He arrived about forty minutes later.

Thomas smiled. "She captured you and then cut you loose on foot?" He was trying to make light of the situation so Killian wouldn't know he had sat up waiting for him.

"No sir, we weren't watching the time, and it got too dark for her to bring me home. She would have had to drive back by herself, and I didn't want her to do that."

They went in, and Killian ate some warmed-over food. He looked down at the food. "Back home, if you were any later than five minutes, your share was up for grabs. I was lucky that everybody was as sick of cabbage and boiled potatoes as I was."

Thomas laughed and bid him good-night.

The next day, Thomas wanted to ride to the ironworks with Patrick and Killian. On the way, Thomas saw a carriage for sale.

He stopped. "Let's take a look," he said. They rode over to the owner, Sledge Thompson, who was working on one of the wheels. Like most carriages, it was black, carried four people in a pinch, and had a top and yellow wheels.

Thomas looked at Killian. "In the winter you'll need a carriage or you'll be soaking wet all the time." Then he turned to Sledge. "How much do you want for it, Sledge?"

Sledge looked at Thomas. "Well, being as it's you, I could let you have it for four hundred dollars."

Thomas looked taken aback. "For a one-hundred-dollar carriage? No, no."

Sledge shook his head once. "I could come down to three hundred dollars, if that will help you."

"I could come up to two hundred dollars, but that's my final price. Take it or leave it."

Sledge winced. "Well, I'm losing money at that price, but I'll let it go for two hundred dollars."

"Will you deliver it to my house?" Thomas asked.

Sledge nodded and walked away.

Patrick looked at Killian. "They go through that every time they buy and sell. You'll get used to it." Killian smiled, and they rode on.

That morning, Killian looked over the rail at the entrance to the jobs building. There was a number seventeen written on the floor. He went back and told Patrick. At lunch, he rode to the store, and Molly was walking in to eat lunch. He sat down beside her with his plate of chicken, rice, and green beans. He looked at her chicken and dumplings and said, "That looks good."

She looked at him. "You don't have to wait until school starts. You can start right away, if you want."

"What about books? Where do I get them?"

"Right here at the store. I'll pick out the ones you will need, and you can come by and pay for them."

"That will work. Where exactly at your house will we study? In your room?"

She gave him a fake look of scorn. "Shh, somebody will hear you. No, we'll be at the dining room table."

"That's going to make it hard to steal a kiss, isn't it?"

"You're there to study, not kiss."

"I don't see why the two can't overlap, do you?"

She giggled. "We'll have to see."

They finished lunch, and Killian went back to work. On the way home, he stopped by to see how much the books would be, and Mr. Anderson told him it would be four dollars. Killian nodded and said, "I'll have the money in the morning."

After arriving at home, he asked Thomas if he could buy the schoolbooks. He said he needed four dollars. Thomas looked surprised. He said to Killian, "Four dollars? What in the hell is she going to teach you?"

Killian laughed.

The next morning, Killian went by the store and gave Mr. Anderson the four dollars. Killian asked if he could pick up the books, and Mr. Anderson told him that Molly had already taken them home.

After work, he rode over to Molly's house, a little apprehensive about her mother. He got down, and Molly came out to greet him. She looked at him and said, "From my window up there, I can see you when you're at the store."

Killian looked up. "So, that's your window, huh?"

She looked at him with a smile. "Yes, why do you want to know?"

"Oh, just in case of a fire, I might have to climb one of those fire ladders to come get you. And if we ever decide to run off, I'll put my own ladder up there and get you."

She took his arm. "You got this all figured out, haven't you? Well, I hate to disappoint you, but we aren't going to have a fire or run off. It's time for school. Come on."

He went in, and they sat down at the dinner table. Molly's mother started out with the food. Molly smiled. "We'll eat first and then study."

"I can't let you do this every night."

Molly looked at him. "I don't see why not. We always have enough in case my uncle comes by."

"Isn't he in Ireland?"

"He's due back today."

Killian had chills and wished Thomas was there to handle the situation. They got to studying, and Killian had a lot of reading to do. When he finished, Molly looked at him. "You read pretty fast, so you must read pretty well," she said.

"I was good at reading, and I like to read. My brothers would bring books home and have me read them and tell them what they were about, so they could go back and convince the teacher that they had read them."

Molly laughed. "Well, this teacher is too smart for that."

Nothing else was said, and the uncle never came by, so Killian was glad of that. Now he could formulate a plan with Thomas. Killian left at eight thirty, rode home, and put his horse up. He carried his book in, lay in his bed, and read. He was supposed to read two chapters, but he read five. He dropped off to sleep with his book on his chest and his clothes on. When he woke up, there was a blanket on him, and the lamp had been turned off. He knew Thomas had done it.

That morning, Thomas asked him, "How was the first day at school?"

"Pretty good, but Molly expects me to eat there every night, and I don't feel good about that. But I guess I could come home and get back there by six, which is the time they get through eating. That's a lot of horse riding for nothing, and in the winter, it's going to be too cold to ride all that way. By the way, she said her uncle was home from Ireland. I didn't see him, but I'm sure I will. Any ideas?"

Thomas shook his head. "I've thought about that a lot, and it depends on what he says. I wish I could be there when it happens, but I can't. Tomorrow or the next day, I want to take you to the gristmill and have you work there for a while."

"Why the change?" Killian asked.

"Why not?"

Killian went back to Molly's house at five fifteen and had dinner. He helped clear the table, and Molly stopped him. "Don't do that. Men don't do the dishes."

"They do if there are no women in the house."

They started studying after the table was cleared. She asked questions to see if he understood what he had read. She was impressed with his answers. "Read the next two chapters, OK?"

169

He smiled. "It was so interesting, I read the first five."

She asked questions about the next three chapters. "If you stay this far ahead, you'll finish before the end of the year." After they finished studying, they walked out on the front porch. She looked at him. "Can I ask you a serious question?"

"Sure, anything."

"Why did you tell me you only had four brothers? My uncle told me you had six. Is that true?"

Killian hadn't expected this to come from her. "Four, six, what's the difference?"

"That's not an answer. Why did you tell me you only had four when you have six? He gave me their names."

Killian looked serious. "What did he say about it?"

"Oh, he just wondered why you told him it was four instead of six. Unlike me, they may not realize you have six uncles and that your father is the seventh and that you are the seventh son of the seventh son. I think I've discovered that mysterious secret that lies deep in your eyes, haven't I?"

"Maybe. Will you talk with my grandfather before you say anything to anybody? There's something else you should know, but he'll need to explain it to you."

She nodded. "I'll go talk to him in the morning, if that's OK. I feel so much closer to you now for some reason, as if we share something. I would love to kiss you right now, but I know my mother is looking."

Killian looked up and at the window. "She is." He bent down and kissed her. "Do you care at this point?"

She shook her head. "Good night." Then she turned and walked in.

When he got home, he told Thomas what had transpired.

Thomas nodded. "You did good, but I still don't know how to handle the uncle. We'll have to see how that turns out."

The next morning when Patrick came to pick up Killian, Thomas scratched his chin. "I'm taking him to the gristmill so he can see how it operates."

Patrick smiled and nodded. "OK, sorry to lose him. He has a lot of good ideas."

"That's good to know. If you have a problem, let the young man have a look at it." Patrick nodded and rode off, and Thomas thought about how Killian had become wise beyond his years and how glad he was that Patrick recognized Killian's gifts.

Thomas saw Molly coming down the road in her cart. He said over his shoulder, "Killian, we have a visitor."

Killian came out and stood there waiting for her. "Sorry, Grandfather. I was brushing my teeth."

Thomas smiled. "It's good to have fresh breath when talking to a young woman."

Molly stopped, and Killian took her hand as she stepped out of the cart. "Good day, Killian, and good day, Mr. O'Rourke," she said. They both acknowledged her.

Killian led her up the steps and said, "Come up here and sit down." He led her to his rocking chair.

"Oh, I wondered when I would get the privilege of sitting in the coveted rocker." She smiled as Thomas did.

Killian stepped down three steps so he would be on the same level and faced them.

Thomas looked at her. "I know you know this, but I want to emphasize the importance of Killian's gift. How much do you know about the seventh son of the seventh son?"

"Well, I read up on it last night, and it has different meanings. He could be considered a gifted person that helps people or a devil worshiper. I learned that he could have a gift or any or all of several gifts."

Thomas smiled. "You're a very smart girl. No matter how good his intentions are, if people discover him, he will be labeled a devil worshiper by those who believe that. When I lived in Ireland, there was a man named Paul Cawley who was hanged because of being the seventh son of the seventh son. If word gets out, Killian will have to leave town—if they don't hang him first. Do you understand?"

She nodded her understanding, and Thomas started to explain that Killian was considered a suspect in the first murder because he was new in town.

As Thomas continued to explain, his voice seemed to drift away where Killian could barely hear him. Killian started seeing flashes of light in his eyes, and everything started growing dim. He felt his knees hit the steps in front of him. He extended his arms and felt them touch the steps.

He heard Thomas saying in a far-off voice, "Killian. Killian, what's wrong?"

He sounded as if he was getting farther away. He could hear Molly doing the same, and she sounded far off too. He felt them put their hands under his arms and lift him. He struggled the best he could and soon felt himself being lowered, and then he was on something soft. He thought he was still on the porch, but they had managed to get him to his bedroom.

He could hear Molly screaming, "We have to get a doctor!"

Thomas shook his head. "No. No doctors yet."

Killian saw total blackness and could no longer hear Thomas or Molly. All of a sudden, he saw a woman lying in the woods. She was undressed from the waist down, and there was a lot of blood around her neck and shoulders. He saw a gravel road in the distance. Then he saw something yellow, and it appeared to be the woman's hat. It had yellow feathers sticking out of it. He felt something patting his cheek and something cool on his face. He could hear Thomas's and Molly's voices again in the distance, and they seemed to be getting closer. He finally opened his eyes and saw Molly looking at Thomas, pleading for him to get a doctor.

Thomas was telling her why he wasn't going to do that.

Killian stuck his hand up between them. "Hey, don't talk about me like I'm dead."

Molly leaned over and kissed him on the mouth, and Thomas had tears in his eyes. "What happened, boy?"

Killian looked at Thomas and back at Molly, not knowing if Thomas wanted him to explain a vision in front of her. Then he realized that she knew everything else about him and she should know this too. He looked at Thomas. "A vision came over me."

Thomas looked shocked. "A vision? But you've never had one while you were awake before. This is something new. What did you see?"

Killian looked at Molly. "You may not want to hear this. It isn't pleasant."

She responded quickly, "Oh yes I do. I'm not leaving, so tell us." Killian told them what he had seen, and when he got to the part about the yellow hat, she gasped.

Thomas looked at her. "Do you know the woman?"

Molly nodded. "There's a guy that my mother wants me to see socially. I have seen him in the company of a woman who frequents one of those places out in the country, you know, where drinking, smoking, and dancing goes on—I've heard. She wore a yellow hat with feathers once when I saw them together."

"Was that the banker and the woman that dressed less than a lady?" Killian asked.

She nodded. "We must get the sheriff," she said.

Thomas stopped her. "That's one thing we cannot do. This may not have occurred yet. He has had visions two days in advance and a week in advance. If you tell the sheriff and it happens later, who do you think they'll blame?"

Molly looked confused. "We have to do something to prevent this."

Thomas shook his head again. "The one thing he can't do is change the future. He cannot interfere, or he will lose his powers. We have to wait. Trust me on this, Miss McGuire." Turning to Killian, he said, "One thing for sure is that you can't go to work, ever. You must always be in the company of me, Paddy, Linda, Alberta…, or Molly."

She smiled at that.

Killian closed his eyes. "I'm so tired," he said. He was soon asleep.

Thomas motioned for Molly to follow him out. He walked out on the front porch and held the door for her. He looked back as she was kissing Killian. She turned and saw Thomas looking, and he smiled and motioned for her with his head. She was relieved that he did not disapprove.

They sat down in the rocking chairs. "If he ever does that while he is with you, explain, if you need to, that the doctors are working with him on the problem, and we don't know what's causing it yet. Then get him back to me as soon as you can." He paused for a moment. "Can you come over here and give him his lessons—for a while at least?"

She frowned. "Father might agree, but Mother never would."

Thomas squinted down the road. "What if I came by and talked with your father. Might he and your mother relent?"

"I don't think so, but it's worth a try."

"Where do you have to be right now?"

"Nowhere, why?"

"I'm going to the ironworks and talk to your father. Will you stay here until he wakes up—on the porch, of course?"

She smiled. "I'll be glad to."

Thomas left, saddled his horse, and went to the ironworks. He walked into the accounting department.

The manager, Mr. Stout, ran over to him. "Mr. O'Rourke, it is good to see you. What can I do for you today?"

"I would like to see Mr. McGuire outside for a minute."

"Yes, sir, and is my presence requested also?" he asked hopefully.

"No, just John McGuire, and be quick about it."

He ran off and reappeared with John and then stood there smiling. Thomas stared at him. "Go back inside, Stout!"

He quickly disappeared.

Thomas put his hand on John's shoulder. "John, my grandson has suffered some kind of ailment. The doctors haven't figured it out yet, but he is going to need to stay off a horse and get plenty of rest. He so wants to complete his education. Could you see your way to letting your daughter come to my house in the afternoons, under my watchful eye, of course, and give him his lessons? She will eat with us, and I or one of my sons will see her to your door every day. I would be grateful if you would."

John pursed his lips. "Mr. O'Rourke, I certainly wouldn't mind, but I'm afraid her mother will never permit it. I'll have to see."

"You're an Irishman. You should make these decisions. But if you must consult your wife, then do so. One more thing: if you permit this, I'll certainly remember it." He looked toward the accounting room and back at John.

John raised his eyebrows. "I'm sure I can convince her. I'll let you know, sir."

Thomas smiled. "Fine, fine, and if that nosy German in there wants to know what we talked about, tell him I have sworn you to secrecy. Or you can tell him it's none of his damn business. I'll protect your job."

John smiled. "That won't be necessary."

Thomas went back home. When he got there, Molly and Killian were sitting on the porch holding hands. Thomas told her what had transpired, and she thanked him.

Molly left, and Killian stayed with his grandfather. Killian wanted to see Molly and knew he had a chance to see her around town—but not after the weekend because she would start teaching next week. Thomas would not agree to let Killian go for a ride because he was afraid Killian would have another vision and fall off his horse.

The next day was Friday, and Molly came driving up with tears in her eyes. Killian ran down to her as Thomas stood up. She almost fell into his arms. When she got to where she could talk, she stopped and looked up at him. "Father came in this morning and said another woman had been murdered out on the Townsend Road. I know it was the one you saw! I just know it!"

Thomas looked mad. "There's nothing we can do. Try to put it out of your mind. Come on in and sit down in the parlor." She went in and sat down, and Killian gave her a handkerchief. Thomas looked at her. "Well, what did your parents say about you coming here to teach?"

She nodded. "Father will allow it, but he had a terrible fight with my mother. I knew she would be against it. She told him if anything happened to me, it would be his fault. Father told her I was a grown woman, and as man of the house, he was making the decision and she had nothing to say about it. They were in their bedroom with the door closed, but I could hear every word." She dried her eyes again.

Killian patted her on the hand. "You should probably go to your mother in a day or two and tell her that you love her and want to respect her wishes, but you feel this is something you have to do. You might add that the reason you and her don't see eye to eye is because you're so much alike."

Molly looked up quickly. "I'm nothing like my mother."

Killian and Thomas both laughed.

Thomas looked at her. "Oh yes you are. You're both strong-willed women and both possess great beauty." He laughed again.

She looked at him. "Thank you, I think."

That brought on another laugh from Thomas.

Molly slowly looked over at Killian and asked, "Why is it you always know the solution to problems? You always know what to say or what to do."

Thomas answered for him. "It is another gift he possesses— wisdom. He thinks older than his years."

Killian added, "Six years older, to be exact."

She smiled at him. "Six?"

Killian looked at her and smiled. "That would make me four years older than you."

She looked at both of them. "What other gifts do you have?"

Thomas sat there, hesitant to tell her. "He has the gift of healing. That is another one that can bring on charges of devil worshiping."

Killian smiled at her. "And sometimes I can tell when a person is not being truthful. Like when a girl tells me she doesn't care about me, I can tell that she does."

Molly smiled, remembering that day. She was grateful that her father had put his foot down to her mother and knew how unusual it was for him to do so.

The next day, Thomas waved Patrick over as he was leaving. He asked, "How's that fellow Stout working out?"

Patrick shrugged. "He gets the job done. Everybody hates him. Killian was right that people will do better work if they are more comfortable. They're not comfortable with him."

Thomas looked down and then back up. "Have you thought about dismissing him?"

Patrick shook his head. "Problem is, he's Linda's uncle."

"Can you reassign him, maybe over those bastards in the boiler room or the jobs room?"

Patrick nodded. "I can do that easily enough. Who would replace him?"

"You'd be doing me a favor if you put John McGuire in that job."

Patrick appreciated that his father was not telling him, but was asking. He nodded and said, "I can do that." Patrick rode off thinking about hiring someone to collect overdue or unpaid debts. He said aloud to no one, "I wonder if he can do that. I could call it a promotion." He rode on, proud of his decision.

The next day, Killian and Molly were studying, and she whispered, "Mother and Father had another argument last night. She told him again that she would hold him responsible if anything happened to me. Father explained again that somebody would see me home, and Mother said she wasn't worried about me coming or going, but rather, she was worried what would happen to me while I was here with you. Afterward, Father took me out on the porch and asked, 'I trust you and Killian, but is there something you need to tell me about your study sessions?' I told him there was. I told him we had kissed several times. He laughed and said, 'OK,' and we went back in."

Killian looked around. "I like your father. He's a smart man. I'll have to work on winning your mother over."

She looked scared. "I won't be able to see you this weekend. I have to prepare all my lesson plans for next week. I'll be back on Monday afternoon."

"You expect me to go two—no, three—whole days without seeing you? I don't think I can make it."

She laughed again. "You'll have to. Look, I don't like it either, but it has to be done or I can't come by Monday."

The next week, Molly came by every afternoon at three fifteen. She ate with them and did lesson plans while Killian studied, until eight thirty, and then either Patrick or Dean would get on his horse and escort her home. They would even put the cart away, tend to the horse, and make sure she got in her door safely. The following weekend was the same. She had to work on her lesson plans all weekend, and Killian didn't get to see her.

Thomas finally took him out in the carriage he had bought, and that broke up the boredom some. In his trips up and down the street in town, he never saw Molly because she was in school.

The next week, Molly was back on Monday. She came Tuesday. On Wednesday when she showed up, she looked tired. "What's wrong, young lady?" Killian asked.

She replied, "Oh, nothing. Just a rough day at school. I'll be all right." Her eyes looked tired, and she had circles under them.

Killian started his assignment. He was way ahead and wanted to stay that way. He finished and looked over at Molly, and she had her head down on the table asleep. Killian looked at Thomas; he was asleep also. He went over and pulled her back from the table without waking her. He picked her up, took her to the couch, and gently laid her down, putting a couch pillow under her head. He got a blanket out of his room and covered her up. She never woke up until he shook her at eight twenty-five.

She jumped up. "Oh, my God. What have I done?" she said.

Killian laughed so loud he woke Thomas. "You fell asleep, so I put you on the couch to rest. Oh, I thought about getting on there with you, but with Thomas being asleep, it didn't seem proper." He looked at Thomas, who was wide-awake by this time.

She started gathering her books. "I'm so embarrassed."

Killian stopped her. "Don't be. There was nothing wrong with your being tired. Now here is what we're going to do. I'm way ahead in my studies, so tomorrow, I want you to go home after school and get some rest. Friday, I want you to do the same. Starting next week, you come by on Tuesday and Thursday. It's not as important for me to be ahead as it is for you to get some rest. We'll slow this whole process down a wee bit."

She smiled affectionately. "Thank you. I'm sorry I'm not up to this." She started to kiss Killian, but Thomas was sitting there.

Thomas saw her. "Excuse me while I see if Patrick is here yet."

When he went out on the porch, Killian gave her a prolonged kiss. He picked up her books and walked her out to her cart.

Thomas nodded. "Well, good night. I'm going to bed." He went back in.

Killian helped her into the cart and kissed her. She looked quickly to see if anybody was watching. About that time, Patrick came over. "Sorry I'm late. I wasn't watching the time."

Killian smiled. "No problem. Good night, Miss McGuire."

She looked back at him. "Good night," and she popped the whip in the air and drove off.

The next day, Killian wished she were coming over, but he knew he had made the right decision. At four o'clock, Killian and Thomas were sitting on the porch and saw a cart coming toward the house at a fast trot.

Mildred McGuire drove up with fire in her eyes. "All right. Where is she?" she asked.

Killian stood up. "She wasn't supposed to come by today," he said.

"She didn't come home."

A chill went over Killian. "I'll get the horses. We have to find her." He ran for the stable. He came back in a few minutes with his and Thomas's horses. Mildred had driven off in a panic.

Thomas looked at the horses. "Why didn't you bring the carriage?" he asked, as he was concerned about Killian.

"Because we may have to split up." As Killian started to put his foot in the stirrup, another chill rippled down his spine, and he felt a little unsteady. He leaned against his horse and without losing consciousness, he had a vision. He could see Molly lying in a bed, asleep and covered up.

Thomas came over to him. "Are you all right? Come on, we have to get you in bed."

183

As he turned to go, Killian stepped up on his horse and rode down the road. Thomas quickly mounted up and followed. Killian rode straight to Molly's house. Mildred was on the front porch, and John had his arms around her.

As they rode up, she turned to Killian with tears in her eyes. "We've sent for the sheriff! She nearly screamed. "And when he comes, I'll have the both of you arrested if any harm has come to her!" She sat on the swing with her head in her hands.

Killian walked up to John. "Did you check her room?"

John frowned. "Her room?"

Killian nodded. He turned and went into the house. A few minutes later, he returned smiling. "She's in her bed, asleep."

Mildred stood up. "Asleep?" She ran in.

John shook his head. "I'm sorry, but how did you know she was in her room?"

Killian laughed. "I didn't. I knew she was tired. So I told her to go home and rest after school. She's safe. We'll be going now." He and Thomas mounted up and rode off.

Thomas looked over at Killian. "I heard what you said to him, but tell me how you knew she was in her room?"

"When I was getting ready to mount up, I saw her in her bed, asleep."

"You had a vision and didn't lose consciousness?"

Killian nodded.

184

The next day, Killian and Thomas walked through the peach orchard, and when they went back to the house about three forty-five, Molly and her mother rode up in the cart.

Thomas looked at Killian. "If you'll excuse me." He started to climb the steps.

Molly cleared her throat and said, "Grandpa Thomas, would you come out here too?"

Mildred looked at Molly when she heard her call him Grandpa Thomas. Thomas walked out and stood by Killian. Molly had a frown on her face, and her arms were crossed. Mildred was looking at the ground, obviously embarrassed. Killian thought it amusing that the daughter had become the mother, and the mother had to play the part of the daughter. Molly nudged Mildred with her elbow.

Mildred inhaled. "I want to apologize." Molly nudged her again, and she looked up at them and continued, "I want to apologize to both of you for my reactions yesterday and for what I said to you. I was worried." Molly nudged her again with her elbow. "I make no excuses for what I did, and I hope you can find it in your heart to forgive me."

Killian nodded. "Forgiven and forgotten."

Thomas just said, "Aye."

Killian looked at Mildred, and she lowered her eyes again, but then she raised them back up before Molly could nudge her.

He held her stare. "Mrs. McGuire, I think enough of your daughter that I would never harm her, body or soul, nor would I let any harm come to her. So if that's what's worrying you, you don't have to worry anymore.

If you think we think enough of one another that we may fall in love someday, you don't have to—" He paused and then corrected himself. "No, you still have to worry about that, I'm afraid."

He saw Molly smile. "Go," he told Molly, "and may the wind be at your back, the sun on your face, and may the road rise up to meet you."

Molly blew him a kiss that her mother didn't see. "Good day to you, sirs," she said. Then they drove off.

The next day, Thomas and Killian took the carriage to the ironworks. When they got to Patrick's office, Thomas said, "Why don't you check on accounting and the jobs department while I go over a few things with Paddy?"

Killian walked downstairs, and as he went down the hall to the accounting department, he saw Mr. Stout in an office by himself with stacks of paper on his desk. He walked on down to accounting and was surprised to see John McGuire at the manager's desk. When he walked in, John greeted him and shook his hand.

"Are you over this department now?" Killian asked.

"Yes, I am. I've been here a couple of days. Didn't your grandfather tell you?"

"No, but I'm not sure he knows. He pretty well leaves it to Patrick to hire the best people." Killian looked out over the men and women at their desks. He saw flowers on some of the desks and photographs of people on other desks, and everybody was smiling.

John stood and said to the people in the room, "Excuse me, everyone. If you didn't know it, this is Killian O'Rourke, Mr. O'Rourke's grandson."

Everybody got up from his or her desk and formed a line to shake his hand.

After they had gone back to work, Killian said in a whisper, "What is Mr. Stout doing? I saw him in an office."

"He is now in charge of collections. You have to be mean to try to collect money, and he fits the job."

They both smiled. Killian shook John's hand again and left.

He walked by the jobs room and saw a sign over the door that read, "Sixteen jobs per shift is our goal." He saw Burt just inside the jobs room with a clipboard in his hand.

Killian walked in to speak to him. "From listening to my uncle and grandfather, you're responsible for this increase in productivity."

Burt's chest swelled with pride. "Well, we must do what we can, don't you agree?"

"Yes, sir. I do. Keep up the good work." He shook Burt's hand and left.

Killian went by the furnace room, and the men all turned and waved. He waved back and went back to Patrick's office. When he got there, Thomas asked him, "Are you ready to go? I'm though here."

Killian nodded. "Did you know John McGuire is head of accounting now?"

Thomas looked surprised. "You don't say."

Patrick asked, "Do you know him?"

Killian nodded. "He's Molly's father."

Patrick looked at Thomas. "You don't say."

Killian thought they both were lying, but he said nothing more.

They drove the carriage to the gristmill, looked around, watching it operate, and then rode to the market. They got home about noon, and Gretchen had lunch ready. Killian read a recent letter from his father, who said all was well and thanked him again for the money.

Thomas looked up from his plate. "How's your father?"

"Oh, says he is doing well. Things are a little better since the drought ended. He says the thirty dollars a month is a life saver for him."

Thomas paused for a moment. "Let's send him fifty dollars a month from now on."

"I appreciate that very much, and I know he will. Can I tell him it's from you? I feel bad to let him think I am working and earning the money."

"No." Thomas paused. "Do you think he would come over here if I paid everybody's way?"

"He said he didn't come when everybody else did because mother didn't want to be separated from her family. But now that she's gone, he might. The only thing stopping him might be if my brothers or my brother's wives refused to come. It's hard to run a farm and feed a family that big without everybody contributing. I think it would have to be everybody or none. You want me to write and ask?"

Thomas just nodded.

The weekend dragged by slower than usual. Killian finally turned to Thomas. "Grandpa, you're going to have to let me go sometime. You can't watch me every minute, and the worst thing that could happen is somebody finds me unconscious. That won't tell them anything about me. Besides, these things come on slow enough that I could get off my horse before I fell off. You have to let me out by myself. People are beginning to think I'm not in my right mind and have to be watched all the time."

Thomas sat there for a while. "I know. I was hoping I could watch you until you married that girl, and then she could watch you." He smiled.

"Well, with that said, I think I'll ride to the schoolhouse for lunch. I should be back by one fifteen or so."

He went in and asked Gretchen if she would fix him a couple of sandwiches to take for lunch. While she was doing that, he filled the canteen up. He saddled his horse and brought it back, and Thomas handed him his lunch. "Don't make me come looking for you," he said with a slight smile.

Killian smiled. "I won't. I'll be all right."

He rode off and soon came up on the schoolhouse. He rode right up front at a few minutes before twelve. He saw Molly look at him and smile. A minute later, she rang the hand bell, and kids came out of the school and headed in twelve different directions.

She walked out on the porch. "What do I owe this surprise to?"

"I convinced Thomas that I needed some freedom. I told him people were thinking I was not in my right mind and couldn't be left alone."

She laughed. "Wait a minute and let me get my lunch." She walked back inside.

He stepped to the door. "I just wanted to see which one of these little desks would be mine if I ever came to class."

She smiled. "Probably a big chair by my desk so I could watch you and make sure you didn't misbehave."

"Oh, you heard about those spitballs in the tenth grade, then."

She laughed again. "No, but it doesn't surprise me. Do you mind if we eat out on the porch?"

"It's all right with me. Are you afraid to be alone with me?"

"No, but these kids see things through their little eyes, and it doesn't always reflect reality. What I mean is, by the time the story gets home to Momma and Daddy, it has a different light on it. Understand?"

Killian nodded. "What have you got for lunch? I might want to swap with you."

She looked at the dish she had. "I'm not sure. It has no smell that I'm aware of, and Mother didn't say what she fixed."

Killian laughed. "Well, Gretchen fixed you a chicken sandwich." He gave her one of his sandwiches.

"Tell Gretchen that I am indebted to her. She seems a lot younger than your grandfather."

190

"She is. She was Grandpa's best friend's wife, and he died a pauper with a lot of debt, and she was put out on the curb. Thomas took her in and married her to keep the town gossips quiet. She has her bedroom in the back, and his is next to mine."

"That's so nice of him. He's really not as fierce and gruff as he lets on, is he?"

"No, you have him pegged right."

She looked at Killian as he ate. "But he would do anything in this world for you."

Killian nodded. "I was pretty close to my father, but not as close as I am to my grandfather. I think my father knew about my birthright and tried to keep me from coming to America. We spent a lot of time talking, and my brothers resented me, I think. Maybe that's why we fought all the time."

"Did you hate your brothers?" She took another bite of her sandwich.

"Oh, no. I love every one of them. Fighting was just a pastime, sort of."

Molly laughed at that.

"We're of a different breed in that regard. I'm an only child, and you have six brothers. What if one had been a girl? Would you still have had six brothers before you became the seventh son?"

"No, it doesn't work that way. It has to be an unbroken line of boys."

"Really?"

Killian nodded and finished his sandwich.

"I'm going to try to come back at three and see you home if Thomas hasn't had a fit over my visit at lunch."

"That's awful nice, but I hate to put you to such a bother."

He looked in her eyes. "It's never a bother to get to see you. I have trouble going a day without speaking to you or seeing you."

"You're so considerate, and I don't see that secret in your eyes, now that I know what it is. It's amazing that I could see something while looking in your eyes. Something was actually there. I love looking into your eyes now. All I see is softness, and they are kind of dreamy too." She smiled as she looked at him.

"Would this be a good time for a kiss?"

"Oh no, if one of the parents over there in one of those houses saw it, I would probably be fired. If one of the kids saw it, I would definitely be fired. The school board is kind of strict."

"Can I come by at three and see you home?

"I guess so. We'll see if I get any backlash from it."

About that time, they heard a little voice say, "Who are you?"

They turned, and there was a little girl about seven. Molly folded her hands on her knee. "Kara, this is my friend, Killian."

Killian smiled, and Kara walked forward and looked at Molly, asking, "Is he your sweetheart?"

Molly smiled. "Well, he's a sweetheart, but he's doesn't belong to me."

She looked at Killian. "Is she your sweetheart?"

Killian winked at her. "She is, but she doesn't know it yet."

Molly nudged Killian with her elbow and in a singsong voice said, "Remember what we talked about?"

Killian raised his head. "Oh yeah, sorry. No, little girl. I just came to sweep the schoolhouse out, but it looks like I will wait until three. See you later." Molly waved and winked at him, and he got on his horse and left. He arrived back at precisely one fifteen. Thomas was sitting on the porch waiting, of course.

Killian went back at two forty-five, but stopped at the top of the hill when he saw a horse and carriage out front. He turned and walked his horse under a tree and sat there. The children let out at three, but the buggy was still there. It left about three twenty, and he saw Molly come out, get in her cart, and start driving in his direction. She didn't seem to be happy at all.

She passed by him. "Meet me at the park, OK?" she said.

He nodded and followed her.

When they got there, he got down and went over to her. "What's wrong? And who was that in the carriage?"

She was almost in tears. "It was Mrs. Tarbell. She accused me of having a man in the school at lunch. I told her you were a student taking the eleventh and twelfth grades, and you came by to get your assignments, and we sat on the porch and went over them. She kept saying she was told we were inside. I told her to tell the old, blind busybody who was snooping to pay better attention because we were not in the schoolhouse. I don't know if she is going to fire me or not." She started crying.

Killian took her hands. "I'm sorry. I won't come down again, and I'm glad I stopped at the top of the hill just now. I'm really sorry."

"You don't have to be sorry; you did nothing wrong. You may have to meet me at the park until it turns too cold to do that."

"I can do that," he said. "I had planned to come to the park every day at three and swing anyway."

She laughed. They talked awhile, and Killian knew that she had to go, and he didn't want to make Thomas uneasy by being away. He was sorry he couldn't kiss Molly good-bye, but there were too many people in the park. She got into her cart and drove off, and he went home.

The next day at three fifteen, he was sitting at the picnic table, and she came walking up. She was trying to smile, but Killian could tell something was wrong. She looked at him, and he looked at her. "OK, let's have it. What's wrong?" he asked.

She lowered her head. "Yesterday when I got home, Mother told me to put on a nice dress because we were having someone over for dinner. When I got downstairs, it was the banker. She had invited him without telling me. I was so mad at her, and I don't think Father liked it, either. After the meal, he sat around telling us all about the banking business. I was bored to tears. Mother even asked if we wanted to sit on the porch, and I told him I had to make a lesson plan and I couldn't. He finally left, and Mother came yelling at me about being rude. For the first time in my life, I yelled back at my mother. I told her if she didn't stop interfering with my life, I was going to move out. I told her never to do that again. She looked at my dad and said, 'Are you going to let her talk to me like that?' He said, 'She's right. If you don't want to be yelled at, treat her with respect. If you invite that fellow back over here, you had better be interested in him, because she's obviously not.'"

"Seriously, did your father say that?"

"Not only that, but they had another big fight in their room after that. I'm sorry, but I must go. I'm not very good company today. Oh, by the way, Mrs. Tarbell came by and told me I couldn't teach anybody who wasn't approved by the school board, and I'm not getting paid by the board for teaching you."

"They pay you by the student?"

She shook her head. "Monthly," she said.

He said, "How much?"

"Twenty-eight dollars a month for the ones I teach now."

He walked her to her cart and watched her drive off. He heard a voice behind him say, "Are you interested in her?"

He turned and found a professional-looking man, a little older than Killian was, in a suit. "What business is it of yours who I am interested in?" Killian asked.

The man smiled. "Well, I intend to marry her."

"You must be that banker she said came to dinner last night."

"I am, and I intend to call on her. I have her mother's permission."

Killian laughed. "You may not know this, but if you marry someone, you have to have her permission too. I don't think you're going to get it from her."

"I bet I get to kiss her before you do." The banker smiled real big.

Killian smiled back. "You would have to kiss her for the next two months to even catch up to me."

The man lost his smile. He cleared his throat. "Nevertheless, I plan to court her, and I have her mother behind me."

Killian looked him in the eye. "I am already courting her, and I have her father behind me."

The banker lost his smile again. "What's your name?"

"What's yours?"

"Harmon Baker Drexler the third."

"My name is Killian O'Rourke the first."

Harmon looked up at the sky. "Where have I heard the name O'Rourke before?"

Killian shrugged. "I don't know, maybe O'Rourke Iron Works, O'Rourke Grist Mill or maybe O'Rourke Market. Pick any of the above."

"Well, your father banks with us. We have all his money."

Killian shook his head. "My father still lives in Ireland. You are referring to my grandfather, Thomas. Say, weren't you keeping company with that woman who was murdered a while back?"

Harmon's eyes got big, and his face got red. "I did not. Who said I was with her? That could get your nose bloodied."

Killian stepped up closer to Harmon. "I have six brothers, and I used to get bloody noses all the time. The likes of you don't scare me. If you want to bloody my nose, have a swing."

The man stepped forward and punched at Killian like a girl, and when he missed and drew his hand back for another shot, Killian hit him with a light shot, right in the nose.

Harmon staggered back and took his handkerchief out. He put it up to his nose and turned to walk away.

Killian watched him walk away. "Hey, Harmon Baker Drexler the third, anytime you want another shot at me, let me know."

As Killian went back to his horse, he realized that he had told the man about his six brothers. "That was not smart," he thought.

Killian went home and told Thomas about the incident. That's when they saw the sheriff riding up the road. He stopped in front of the porch. "Killian, I have a man that says you hit him unprovoked. Is that true?"

Killian shook his head. "I didn't. He punched at me first and missed."

The sheriff looked down. "Well, he has an important father in this town who wants you arrested."

"I have an important grandfather in this town who doesn't want me arrested."

The sheriff looked reluctant. "He has a witness that says you punched him too."

"He's lying, Sheriff. Harmon stopped me in the park and told me to stay away from Molly. That he was going to marry her. I told him that he wasn't—not without her say-so."

"I'm going to have to take you in. Your grandfather can bail you out in a couple of hours."

Thomas stood up. "You idiot. You think that banker is going to get you reelected? The people will vote you in—or out—as the case may be."

The sheriff took out a set of handcuffs, and Killian stood up. "I'll go with you, but if you try and put those on me, you're going to have to fight me first."

The sheriff looked at him and said, "Go get your horse."

Thomas said to the sheriff, "Go on back to the jail. I'll bring him in."

The sheriff nodded and left.

Thomas told Killian to get the carriage, and they went to the jail. On the jail's front porch was Harmon, his father, and another man about Harmon's age. When Killian got out, he looked at the men. "Who is this other person I supposedly hit?"

The young man stepped forward and said, "Me." He smiled.

Killian stepped up and looked at him in the light. "If I had hit you, your nose would be swelled up as big as his. You don't have a mark on you."

The man smirked. "Yes, I do. You see the mark beside my nose?"

Killian leaned in. "Let me look."

When the man turned his face toward him, Killian punched him square in the nose. His head went back and hit the porch post. His nose was bleeding from the punch, and his head was bleeding from hitting the post. The man slid to the floor and fell off the porch.

Killian looked at the sheriff. "Now you can arrest me. I'll admit to hitting him first." He looked at Harmon. "You and I will meet again, so be looking for me." He walked into the jail.

Two hours later, Killian was let out of jail on a seventy-five dollar bond.

On the way home, Thomas looked at Killian. "We have to play this smart. This is not Ireland. You can't beat up everybody you have a squabble with."

"Yes, sir, I know. I'm sorry for the inconvenience."

Thomas grinned at Killian's stubbornness. "It's no bother."

They had to be in court at ten the next morning. Killian wore his good clothes and had his hair combed nice. He sat down near the front, and Thomas sat in the back. Killian saw Harmon and the other man walk in. The other guy had a swollen nose and a big bandage around his head. Killian started to get worried. When they were called, Harmon and his friend each went to the stand and told their lies. Then Killian was called up, and the judge asked him if he had hit the two men.

Killian admitted he did.

The judge looked at him. "Well, why don't you tell me the details?"

Killian told him of meeting a young lady in the park. He told of Harmon coming up behind him and informing him that she was his girl and that he planned on marrying her. "We talked like gentlemen, and when I asked him if he was keeping company with that last woman who had been murdered, he said he was going to bloody my nose. He swung and missed. I swung and didn't."

The sheriff and judge looked at Harmon when Killian said that.

"When we got to the jail, that other jaybird said I had hit him also, but he wasn't even there. I told him he didn't have a mark on him, so I put one on him for lying. I was going to go to jail for hitting him anyway, so I owed him. He dropped like an old lady."

The judge was trying to keep from laughing. He looked at the two men. "Mr. Drexler III, you work at the bank. Is that correct?"

He stood up. "Yes, sir. We both do."

The judge nodded. "So you're coworkers and friends, is that correct?"

Harmon nodded as he smiled. "Yes, sir, good friends.

The judge looked over the top of his glasses. "I see." He looked at Killian.

"Mr. O'Rourke. You don't work, is that correct?"

"Yes, sir, I do. I sort of float between the ironworks, the gristmill, and the market, wherever they need me the most."

The judge nodded again. "I see. What we have here is two young men that got into fisticuffs over a young lady. This happens more often than not, I suppose. Mr. Harmon, I have doubts about your witness, so I'm going to call this one even. Now, since Mr. Harmon has the injuries, as does his witness, I am going to charge Killian with assault. I going to sentence him to two months in jail and fine him one hundred dollars. I'm going to suspend the sentence and put him on probation for two months."

Harmon's father jumped up. "This is outrageous. This man ought to be sentenced to two years in prison."

The judge stared over his glasses at Mr. Drexler. "Mr. Drexler, don't tell me how to run my court and I won't tell you how to run your bank. Before I pass sentence, is there anybody who's got anything to add?" he said, looking at the two parties.

Thomas stood up in the back. "Judge, I would like to know if the senior Drexler would persuade the young Drexler to drop the charges."

Mr. Drexler looked back. "Thomas, is this one of your boys?"

Thomas nodded. "He's my grandson, fresh from Ireland, where young men settle their differences rather than bother the authorities."

The older Drexler looked at the judge. "One moment please." He went and talked to his son. Harmon kept shaking his head and everybody heard Mr. Drexler raise his voice. "If you don't, both of you will be out of a job tomorrow." He turned to the judge. "Your honor, my son agrees to drop the charges."

The judge looked at Harmon. "Is that right, young man?" he asked. Harmon sat there seething and finally nodded his head. The judge hit his gavel on the desk. "In that case, the trial is dismissed."

As they walked out, Killian asked Thomas, "Why did he do that? How did you know he would?"

Thomas looked over and smiled. "Because if I take my money out of his bank, it would collapse."

They started toward the carriage, and the senior Drexler walked up. "Mr. O'Rourke, you owe me big time on this. Your boy should have gone to jail for two years, and if it happens again, he will." He began to walk away and then turned back. "And if he mentions any association with that murdered woman and my son again, you'll hear from my lawyer. Mark my words on that."

They got in the carriage and started home. As they approached the park, Killian saw Molly in her cart heading for school. "Grandpa, pull up there and let me talk to her a minute." He jumped out. "Molly, wait!" he called out.

She stopped about twenty yards away. He ran up there and saw the frown on her face. "What's wrong?" he asked.

She looked at him with her eyes narrowed. "You beat those two boys because one said he was interested in me? How could you? I don't want to see you again. All you know is fighting. Well, I'm not going to be associated with anybody who thinks like that." She looked straight ahead.

Killian shook his head. "Next time, you might want to get both sides of the story before you charge someone, find them guilty, and stand them up to be shot."

She looked at him. "You didn't hit Harmon?"

"After he swung at me!"

Without looking at him, she said, "I'll have your books delivered to your house."

"Keep them!" He turned and walked away.

He and Thomas went back home, and then Killian sat on the porch, staring into space.

Thomas looked over. "I'm going to the ironworks. Do you want to go?"

"No, sir. I'll be here when you get back."

Thomas nodded, got into the carriage, and left. Killian was so mad he wanted to punch something or somebody, but he thought better of it because that was what got him into trouble in the first place.

Thomas came back a few hours later and sat there. He looked at Killian. "You've never lied to me, and I don't want you to start now. Did you swing first at the Drexler boy?"

Killian looked him in the eye. "No, sir. He said he was going to bloody my nose and swung at me. I hit him before he could swing again."

"OK, I believe you. Now, was that other boy there at the time?"

"No, sir. The first time I saw him was at the sheriff's office, and I know I shouldn't have hit him, but I was going to jail for it anyway, so I took a shot."

Thomas looked serious. "If I know old man Drexler, he'll come after you some other way. Some way that we won't think it's him. I'm sorry about the girl. She is nice, but if she's not there at a time like this, there's a good possibility she won't be there when you need her the most."

Killian just nodded.

Chapter 11

The next few weeks were torture for Killian. He was so angry, he couldn't see straight. He talked to Patrick about putting him in the furnace room. Patrick agreed. Killian went to the ironworks with Patrick, got a scoop, and shoveled coal all day long. He kept up with the two men on either side of him. At the end of the shift he could hardly move, he was so sore.

When he got home covered in coal dust, Thomas stood up and looked at him. "What in the hell have you been doing?"

"I started work today. I started in the furnace room shoveling coal."

He could see that Thomas was mad, and he told himself that he didn't care, but he realized that he did. His grandfather meant more to him than anybody had since his mother died.

The next morning, Patrick came by Thomas's house. "Find some other place to work," he told Killian.

Killian looked puzzled. "I thought we agreed that I should start at the bottom and work my way up."

"Yeah, we agreed on that, but I'm not going to incur the wrath of my father so you can work out your frustrations. Find somewhere else to work."

Killian didn't blame his grandfather for doing what he did. He really wanted to please the old man. He went into the house suddenly exhausted, not only from the furnace room but because he hadn't slept much since the incident with Harmon. He took a bath, went to his bedroom, and fell across the bed. He felt as if he had fallen a hundred feet and still hadn't hit the bed. He finally stopped falling and saw a woman lying dead. There was blood all over her. He could see the back of Thomas's house through the woods. He looked back down at the woman and woke up.

He struggled to get up and staggered to Thomas's room, but he wasn't there. He walked out on the front porch and found Thomas in his rocking chair.

Thomas looked around. "You're finally up," he said.

Killian looked at him in wonderment. "You haven't gone to bed yet?"

Thomas looked at him. "You've been asleep for twenty hours. I assume you were tired."

"I fell on the bed and fell hundreds of feet, and when I stopped, I saw a dead woman. When I looked through the branches of the trees, I could see the back of our house."

Thomas looked behind him as if he could see through the house. "What? You saw this in a vision?"

"I guess, but I felt like I had been gone for five minutes, maybe three. You said I've been asleep for twenty hours?"

Thomas nodded.

Thomas told him to saddle the horses. Killian came back with the horses, and they got on.

Thomas kicked his horse. "See if you can find the spot. If we happen upon the body while out riding, they can't pin it on you."

They rode out, and Killian kept looking back trying to get the angle he saw in his vision. He kept riding to the left.

Thomas asked, "Are you sure?"

Killian kept going without answering.

He finally looked back. "We're just about there," he said. He rode behind a low-growing tree, and there she was, just as in his vision. He kept trying to keep from getting sick, but wasn't able. He leaned over and threw up off the side of his horse.

Thomas rode over to him. "Ride through those trees that way, and you should come out near the road the sheriff is on. Get him and hurry back."

Killian took off at a gallop. After ducking tree branches and riding around thickets with thorns, he came out on the road. He marked the spot he came out at and rode to the sheriff's office.

"Sheriff!" he called out.

The sheriff came out. "Grandpa and me were out riding, and we came across a dead woman."

The sheriff turned to his deputy. "Jimmy, get a wagon ready." Then to Killian, "Show me." He followed Killian.

Killian took him back the way he had come, and they finally saw Thomas sitting on his horse. As they rode up, Thomas held up his hand to

Killian, so he stopped. The sheriff got off and looked. He looked at the body and then at Thomas. "What happened over there?" he asked.

Thomas looked in that direction. "The boy got sick when he saw the body. It was his first."

The sheriff looked at the dead woman. "Can you send him for the wagon and lead them back in through your property?"

Thomas rode over to Killian. "Go back and lead the wagon around to the house, and when you get to the house, you stay there."

Killian nodded and rode back. He took the wagon and the three men on it down the road to the house and pointed in the direction of the body. They continued on. He started to get down when he saw Molly's cart coming.

She pulled up. "Can I talk to you?" she asked. She still had that look on her face that she'd had when she told him she didn't want to see him again.

He looked at her and said, "No." Then he turned and followed the wagon.

When he got down near the body, Thomas came riding out at a fast pace. "I told you to stay at the house," he said.

"I know, but Molly came down and wanted to talk to me, and I don't want to talk to her."

Thomas sighed. "OK, but stay here. You don't want to see this."

Killian nodded.

He waited about fifteen minutes and started back to the house. She was gone when he got there, so he tied his horse up out front and went into the house. He lay on the bed and fell into a vision. He saw a woman lying facedown. He saw no blood. He looked hard through the trees and saw a red flag. He tried to look closer, and he woke up. He got up and went out on the porch and found Thomas was sitting in his chair.

Thomas looked around. "I'm glad you are finally up."

Killian sat down. "Did they get the body out?"

Thomas looked at him for a minute. "Yes. Yesterday."

"Yesterday? We just found her this morning."

"No, you have been asleep for almost sixteen hours. Did you have another vision?"

Killian nodded. "I saw a woman lying facedown in the woods, but there was no blood this time. I could see a red flag through the trees."

"Red flag? I don't know of any red flags around here. Anything else?"

"No, sir, just woods."

Thomas stared off in the distance. "There's no telling where it is. Looks like you got company coming."

Killian looked, and Molly had just turned the corner. He turned to go back inside. "Tell her I don't want to see her."

She drove up. "Thomas, is Killian here?" she asked.

"He doesn't want to see you, Molly. I'm sorry."

"Why? I need to know some things."

Thomas looked at her. "Well, he figured you prejudged him without getting his side of the story. He figured if you weren't going to believe him about that, you wouldn't believe him when he needed you the most. I think you know what he means by that."

She nodded and drove off. After she had turned the corner, Killian came back out.

"Thanks, Grandpa," he said.

Thomas turned to him as he sat down. "She wouldn't hear you out when you tried to explain to her, would she?"

"No, sir, she wouldn't, and I'm not forgetting that."

"Seems like you remembered it well, because that's what you're doing to her, ain't it?"

Killian didn't say anything. He sat there staring off into space.

It got dark, and Thomas looked at him. "Aren't you going in?" he asked.

"I'm scared to sleep."

"You're going to have the vision even if you don't sleep. Go to bed."

"I know, but lately, I've lost a day every time I slept."

"Still, go to bed and try to rest."

Killian went to sleep and woke up the next morning feeling better than he had in a while.

He got up and put his clothes on. He started for the door and heard Molly's voice. He peered out the door, and she was sitting in his rocking chair talking to Thomas. He heard her say, "I don't blame him for being mad at me, but if I meant as much to him as he said I did, I can't see him not speaking to me again."

Thomas looked over. "He doesn't know this, but my sons tell me they've seen you around town with this Drexler guy. That's going to hurt when he finds out. You not only wouldn't listen, but have taken up with the guy who tried to put him in jail for two years. I'm not saying you abandoned him, but he feels that way."

Molly looked down. "If he would just listen."

"I don't understand young people. You wouldn't listen to him when he needed you to, and now he won't listen to you when you need him to. I can't make him talk to you and wouldn't if I could. He has to come to that decision himself. What about this other guy. Are you sweet on him?"

Molly shook her head. "No, I first started seeing him because I was so mad at Killian. My mother has been pushing him on me for a long time. I don't care about him."

"He told Killian that he was going to marry you and he had your mother on his side."

"He what? That's ridiculous. I would never marry him."

"Between him, your mother and you running around with this guy, what's Killian supposed to think?"

"I'll tell Harmon that I'm never going to see him again."

211

Thomas looked sideways. "You better tell your mother also."

She nodded. "Tell him I want to talk to him, please."

"I'll tell him." She got in her cart and rode away.

Killian went back down the hall to get breakfast, so Thomas wouldn't know he'd been listening. Gretchen fixed his breakfast, and he was eating when Thomas came into the kitchen. "Did you know Molly was here to see you again?"

Killian looked up over his eggs. "Really? This morning?"

Thomas nodded. "I think you should go and talk with her. I really do."

"Why?"

Thomas looked at him. "Because you're in love with her," he said.

Gretchen smiled over her shoulder.

Killian sat there a minute, and the weight of what Thomas had said settled on his shoulders. He nodded and got up and saddled his horse. He rode out and turned toward the park. When he got there, he saw Molly standing by the picnic table talking to Harmon. He started to ride by and let her see him, but instead got off his horse and walked straight toward them. As he got near them, he said to Molly, "I hear you wanted to see me."

She turned quickly toward him. "Yes, will you listen?"

Harmon looked at Killian. "I can't leave you with him, Molly. Your mother wouldn't like it."

She turned her head. "Harmon, please leave. I need to talk to Killian."

He shook his head. "I can't let you go with him."

"You have nothing to say about it, Harmon. Now please leave."

Harmon looked at her. "What do you see in this guy? He has to have a babysitter with him all the time. Now, Killer, or whatever your name is, take your Irish ass out of here before you get punched out."

Molly stepped between them. "No, don't fight, and for your information, I have an Irish ass also."

Harmon stepped past Molly and hit Killian in the nose. Killian stood there and let him. He stood there with blood running down his nose. Killian looked at him. "Is that all you got?" he said. "You punch like a girl. Let me show you what it feels like to be punched out by a man." He stepped forward and heard a voice.

It was the sheriff. "What's going on here? Why did you hit him?"

Harmon looked at the sheriff. "I didn't hit him."

Molly turned to the sheriff. "He did too. I saw him."

The sheriff steadied his gaze on Harmon. "It doesn't matter. I saw it, and I am the one that counts. Come on, son. You'll get the same treatment he got." The sheriff led him away.

Killian looked at her. "Now, what is it you need to see me about?"

Molly looked around; a lot of people were watching. She looked down and then up at him. "I had to let you know something." Tears started pouring down her cheeks. "I love you and can't live without you, and I'm sorry."

He walked over, picked her up, and kissed her, long and hard. The crowed started applauding. He set her back down on her feet, and she had blood under her nose from his. He led her back to his horse, picked her up, and put her on the back. He climbed into the saddle and walked the horse over to Molly's cart. He reached down and grabbed the hitch rope on her pony, and it followed behind. He walked his horse to her house with her holding tightly to him. He stopped in front of her house and slid down. He put his hands on her waist and lowered her, and when she got even with his face, she put her arms around his neck and kissed him.

She didn't stop when her mother screamed, "Molly Malone McGuire, stop that and get in here!"

Killian smiled. "Molly Malone?"

"Shut up. Don't make fun of my middle name."

"I'm glad you don't know mine."

"What is it? Tell me."

Her mother raised her voice. "Molly, come here."

"Be quiet, Mother; I'm busy."

Her mother stamped her foot. "For your information, young lady, Harmon should be here any minute."

Without taking her eyes off Killian, she said, "No, he won't. He's in jail."

Mildred came around the horse. "Jail? For what?"

214

Molly looked at her. "For hitting Killian. And Killian didn't hit him back."

Mildred looked at Killian's red, swollen nose and bloody shirt.

Molly took his hand. "Come inside. I need to clean you up some," she said.

Mildred put her hands on her hips. "I'd rather he not come in."

Molly and Killian walked by her without taking their eyes off each other. She sat him down at the kitchen table, got a wet cloth, and put it to his nose. She wiped his face off and kissed him. Her mother walked out in frustration.

They heard her say, "I'm glad you're home. Your daughter has been standing out in the street in broad daylight kissing this...this...person. They had Harmon put in jail for something."

John walked into the room and looked at Killian. Then he reached over and shook Killian's hand. Mildred stood there with her mouth open.

John stepped up to Killian. "I understand that the other day, you hit Harmon after he swung at you. I heard from witnesses that his friend wasn't even there."

"Yes, sir, that's the way it happened."

"Did you say Harmon is in jail? For what?"

"For hitting him. Look at his nose." Molly smiled with pride. "Father, I'm thinking I want to find me a place to live on my own." She looked at her mother.

John walked by his wife. "If my daughter moves out, you're moving out too." He went upstairs.

Mildred stood there for a minute with her mouth open. "John, surely you don't mean that." She followed him up the stairs.

Killian kissed her. "See you today for class at my house?" She nodded and kissed him again. He rode home looking forward to class that afternoon.

When she got to his house at three fifteen, she put her hands on her hips. "Now, your first assignment is to tell me your middle name."

He smiled. "Never in a thousand years would I tell you."

She looked at Thomas, who shook his head. "I have no idea. I didn't know he was born until he showed up at my door."

She looked at Killian. "Do you want a failing grade for today? Tell me your middle name."

Killian hesitated. "No laughing."

She nodded.

"It's Gilhooley."

Molly and Thomas broke out laughing.

Killian stood up. "Hey, you said you wouldn't laugh. I get double credit then."

She looked at him, trying to stop laughing. "I'm sorry. Is it for real?"

He nodded.

"Where did you get such a name?"

"It was my mother's maiden name. My father gave it to me so I would use Killian. That's also why I fight a lot. Now how's that, Molly Malone McGuire?"

Thomas laughed again.

The next day, Killian went by the courthouse where Harmon stood in front of the judge. The judge looked at Harmon. "OK, the shoe seems to be on the other foot. Now, what happened?"

After the sheriff got through explaining it, the judge looked out over the courtroom and asked, "Is Killian O'Rourke in the room?"

Killian stood up in the back. "Yes, sir."

Harmon and his father looked back.

The judge looked at him. "Well, do you want to tell your side?"

Killian responded. "It doesn't matter, your honor. I don't want to press charges."

The judge nodded. "Well, this is a little different situation since the sheriff witnessed it. The sheriff can still prosecute, if he wants to. How about it, Sheriff? What do you want to see done?"

The sheriff looked back at Killian. "If he doesn't want to press charges, then I don't either."

The judge hit his gavel on the bench. "Case dismissed. You're free. And gentlemen? Try to stay away from each other. Which one of you is this girl keeping company with?"

Killian raised his voice a little, "Me, your honor." He smiled when Harmon looked back.

As they walked out, Killian stepped up to Mr. Drexler. "Sir, my grandfather doesn't owe you anything anymore."

Drexler nodded and walked out with Harmon, whose nose was still swollen.

The next Thursday at class, Molly looked at him shyly. "Why don't you meet me at the park about noon on Saturday, and I'll bring a picnic lunch."

"Better than that, why don't I pick you up at your door and take you to the park—in a carriage, of course."

She smiled. "That will be good."

"I'll be there at eleven thirty sharp. Does your mother own a gun?"

She laughed real big. "No."

Saturday came, and Killian pulled up front at eleven thirty sharp. He noticed another carriage out front, but knocked on the door anyway. Mildred came to the door. "Molly is busy at the moment. Please come back later." She started to shut the door.

Killian stuck his foot in the door. "Now, Mildred, are we going to fight over this?"

Mildred looked shocked. "How dare you address me by my first name? You should have more respect than that."

"When you start showing me some respect, I'll return it. Now where's Molly?"

218

He heard Molly's voice. "Mother, if that's Killian, you better let him in."

John came in the back door when she said that. "What's going on in here?"

Mildred folded her arms. "Harmon got here first to visit Molly, and then Killian shows up, insults me, and refuses to leave. He stuck his foot in the door so I couldn't close it."

John looked at Killian.

Killian shrugged and said, "That's pretty much all true, except Molly and I had planned on going on a picnic, and I'm here to get her."

John looked into the kitchen. "Harmon, come in here, please."

Harmon walked in, and John faced his daughter. "Molly, do you want to see Harmon today?"

She shook her head. "No, Father. I don't wish to see Harmon ever again."

"Do you wish to see Killian today?"

"Yes, Father. I'm in love with him, and I want to see him whenever I can."

John turned back to Harmon. "Harmon, my daughter has made her choice. Now I ask you to leave my house and not return unless you're coming to see me or my wife. Do you understand?"

As he walked out, Harmon said to Mildred, "Why did you tell me to come over here?" When he got out the door, everybody looked at Mildred. She turned and walked upstairs.

219

John kissed his daughter on the forehead. "You two go ahead, and I'll deal with your mother."

Molly resumed putting things into the picnic basket, and they heard a door slam upstairs. They heard John say, "Why do you keep interfering with her life? Just leave her alone. She's old enough to make her own choices."

They heard Mildred say, "I'm just trying to look out for her, to get her a husband with some prospects. That boy down there is living off his grandfather. When the old man dies, he'll have nothing."

John's voice sounded serious. "Nothing but love, and she won't have that if she marries Harmon. If she marries Killian, they will be just like us when we married. I had nothing, and I was surprised when you said you'd marry me. All we had was love."

Molly was slowly putting things in the basket.

Killian asked, "Have you ever told them you can hear everything down here?"

She cut her eyes over at him. "No, I've been using that to my advantage since I was a small girl."

About that time, they heard the bed squeak. Molly threw a pair of napkins into the basket. "Now it's time to go." She picked up the basket and walked out, leading Killian, who was laughing.

They got to the park and found a nice place in the sun. With fall not far away, it was getting cooler. She spread the cloth on the ground and put the basket down. The sun felt warm on their faces. Before she sat down, Killian took her by the shoulders and turned her to face him. "Have I told you that I love you?"

She smiled real big. "No. You never have, and I was going to mention that to you today."

"Well, I do. I love you very much. I put a lot of stock in what my grandfather says. The last time you came by and I wouldn't see you, he told me that I should go and talk to you. I asked him why, and he said, 'Because you're in love with her.' I already knew that, but that sort of made it a reality."

She looked around and kissed him quickly. "I'll have to thank him for such sound advice."

They sat down and started eating. They talked about the future and the past and reminisced about the first time they met. She put a piece of chicken in his mouth, and he put a carrot in her mouth, and they chewed as if that was the only way they could eat.

When they finished, Killian looked around. "It's such a nice day. Let's take a walk," he said.

They put the picnic basket in the carriage and walked around the park, talking. She had her arm in his, and no one who saw them would doubt that they were in love.

They walked down the street toward the store and met a woman who was carrying a baby and leading two small children. The little girl was screaming. Molly walked up and asked, "Mrs. Childress, whatever is the matter with Mary Margaret?"

Mrs. Childress was almost in tears. "I don't know. She's been crying like this for hours. I'm on the way to the doctor's office now."

Molly stooped down to the little girl. "Let us help you with them."

Mrs. Childress sobbed. "I'd be so grateful. Having three this small is a handful."

Molly reached for Mary Margaret, but Killian stopped her, saying, "Let me have her." He picked her up.

"Now, now. What can the trouble be, little girl?" he said.

She stopped screaming so hard, and Killian asked her mother, "Would you mind if I rubbed her stomach a little?"

The woman shook her head. Killian kneeled down with her on his knee and stuck his hand under her shirt. He could feel the heat. It kept getting hotter, and then finally it started cooling down. She quit crying and just made little huffing sounds.

Mrs. Childress looked scared. "What did you do to her? How did you make her stop?"

"I didn't do anything but rub her stomach. That made her burp a couple of times. She just had a little gas is all."

He stood up with Mary Margaret in his arms and said, "We'll take you back home." They walked to the carriage, and they drove the family home. Mrs. Childress kept thanking them.

They left, and Killian didn't say anything about his hand. It looked burned, but it didn't hurt. He kept it hidden from Molly.

They were driving back toward the park when Killian pulled the reins up quick, and the horse stopped.

Molly almost screamed, "What's wrong with your hand?"

Killian stared straight ahead. "Nothing."

"How did you burn it? It must hurt terribly."

"No, it's OK. Look, it doesn't hurt." He hit his hand with the other one, but he was staring down the street.

Molly looked down the street. "What are you looking at?"

"That red flag on the front of the store. Why is it there?"

Molly laughed. "There's a new food store opening down the road a couple of miles, and Mr. Kellerman said he wanted to make his place a little more festive. See, there's a yellow one on the other side."

"I have to get you home. I have to go see Thomas." He slapped the horse with the reins.

"Killian, what is it?"

"I had another vision of a dead woman, and it had a red flag in it. Let me tell Thomas, and I'll come back by and tell you what we've decided to do. OK?"

She grabbed his arm. "I want to come with you."

Killian agreed and trotted the horse all the way home. He jumped off the carriage, and Thomas could see that something was wrong.

"Mr. Kellerman has a red flag in front of his store."

Thomas motioned. "Go saddle the horses. Molly, will you stay here on the porch?"

She nodded. When Killian got back, they mounted up and rode back to town. They stopped by the store, and Killian said, "It has to be over there." He pointed to the trees across from the store.

Thomas looked around. "I don't want anyone to see us go in the woods here. Let's ride down a bit and come up from the other way."

They rode down to Molly's street, turned, and then went into the woods before they got to the first house. The woods soon got so thick that they had to get off and walk. Killian was looking through the trees at the flag, trying to get the angle that was in his vision.

Thomas stopped. "There she is."

Killian looked, and there was the woman he'd seen in his vision. She was in the same position.

Thomas turned back. "Let's get out of here," he said.

They backed out, got on their horses, and rode back. On the way back, Thomas looked over. "There's not much smell yet, so it had to have happened last night. The thing is, what do we do? If we wait until the body decays, someone will smell it and alert the authorities. If we tell the sheriff, he's going to wonder why we were the ones who found two bodies."

They rode back and told Molly what had happened. She was concerned because it was near her house. She looked at them and said, "What if I tell the sheriff I saw a woman go in the woods and not come out?"

Thomas nodded. "It might work. I hate to get you involved in this."

"I'm already involved, knowing about Killian. Take me home, and I will get my cart and go to the sheriff."

Thomas looked at her. "Tell him you saw her go in yesterday, in case they can tell she's been there a few hours."

Killian touched her shoulder. "If you would rather not do this, we can think of something else."

She reached up and touched his face. "I'll be fine. I can do this."

They took her back, and she got her cart and drove out. Thomas and Killian went to the store to eat and watch. About twenty minutes later, they saw Molly with the sheriff right behind her. About forty minutes later, the sheriff rode back at a gallop.

Thomas stood up. "I'm going back to the house. You go check on Molly."

Killian rode to Molly's door slowly, so as not to draw attention to himself. He got off and knocked. Mildred let him in, and Molly was lying on the couch with a wet rag over her face.

Killian asked, "What happened?"

Molly looked up at him. "I saw a woman go in the woods yesterday and not come out. I told the sheriff, and he went in there and found a dead body." She gagged as she said the word "body."

Killian took the cloth and bathed her face. He grabbed her by the shoulders and said, "Let's get out and get some fresh air."

He went out and hitched her cart up, leaving his horse at her house. They rode around, and the fresh air seemed to revive her. They stopped on the back edge of the park, and they saw Mrs. Childress waving at them. She had her baby with her. They went over, and she looked at Killian rather menacingly, asking, "What did you do to my little girl?"

"I didn't do anything to her. She looks fine."

Mrs. Childress turned to the little girl. "Look at this." She raised the little girl's shirt, and there was a perfect outline of his hand.

She looked over at Molly. "It looks burned, but she's in no pain."

Molly smiled. "Mrs. Childress, I know him. He's no magician or miracle worker. He's just a man. A mighty handsome man, I might add." She smiled at Killian.

The woman didn't look satisfied with the answer. "I'm still worried about—"

Killian knew she wanted to say, "devil worshiper," so he locked eyes with her. "Let's use common sense and not let our emotions tell us what to do. Is she well?"

Mrs. Childress nodded.

"Is she different in any way?"

She shook her head.

"Why don't you be thankful for a wonderful, healthy child? If you need to do something, go to church, get on your knees, and thank God for that. That's all you need to be concerned about."

Mrs. Childress gave a frightened nod, muttered, "Thank you," and left.

Killian was aware that something in his innermost being told him when to be bold enough to tell someone what to do.

Molly put her hand on his face. "You can't do that again. I hate that, but this may expose you. Are you going to tell Thomas?"

"No, I'll let you do that."

"Thanks. He'll probably blame me." She looked at him and smiled.

"No, he won't. He'll be thankful that you were with me."

They drove back to Killian's house. Killian walked up the steps and fell into the chair. He closed his eyes and was soon asleep.

Thomas looked over at him. "What happened to him? Did he have another vision while he was out?"

Molly shook her head. "No. I wish it were that simple." She explained to him what had happened. About that time, the sheriff rode up.

"Thomas, I need to talk to you. I don't know if you want others hearing this or not." He looked at Molly.

Thomas glanced over at Molly. "She can hear. What is it?"

"There's a rumor floating around town about the proximity of these murders to your house. All of them, except the one on the Townsend Road, sort of make a circle around your house. Look at this map."

Thomas and Molly looked at it, and Molly looked up at the sheriff. "They circle my house, too, sheriff. In fact, they could circle a lot of houses."

The sheriff nodded. "That's true, but the rumor is about Thomas's house."

Thomas looked down the street. "Who's spreading the rumors?"

"I don't know. I've been trying to track the source down. One thing, I don't think you or the boy had anything to do with them. That's why I brought the word about this and the map to you. By the way, what's wrong with the boy? Is he asleep?"

"Yeah, he's tired. Now, why do you believe me?"

The sheriff glanced at Killian again. "The boy got sick when he saw that body behind the house. If he had anything to do with it, he would've been used to it. That won't mean much if it ever gets to court, though."

Thomas cut his eyes over to the sheriff. "There's two ways to track down a rumor. The authorities can bring the people in and make them tell who told them. Then you get that person in and you keep on it until you get to the source. The other way is for someone to find that person and beat it out of him. I'll let you handle it for now."

The sheriff nodded and left, knowing that Thomas was telling him to find source of the rumor or he would. Patrick walked up about that time, so Thomas asked him to take Molly home and bring Killian's horse back.

Killian woke up after they had left and smiled. "I need a job. I have to buy a wedding ring."

228

Thomas looked at him. "I'll give you the money, and remember, your job is being the seventh son of the seventh son."

Killian looked back. "How much does that pay, exactly?"

"It pays one hundred a month. You don't do anything but that. Do you understand? And will you obey your grandfather?"

Killian nodded.

Thomas motioned and said, "Come with me."

Killian followed his grandfather to his room. The old man took a key from around his neck and unlocked a trunk in the back of his closet. It was an old, well-worn trunk with brass fittings. Thomas opened it, took out a case, and opened that. He took out three rings. They were his and Killian's grandmother's rings.

He looked over at Killian. "You would do me a great honor if you would use these to be wed in."

Killian was choked with emotion, and a tear started down his cheek. He looked at Thomas. "It would be me that would be honored. Thank you for this. I love you, Grandfather."

The old man broke down and cried as he sat down on the bed. He looked at Killian. "Always tell the ones you love that you love them. Never take it for granted." Thomas tried to say, "I love you," but he broke down and cried every time he tried.

Chapter 12

Two days later, Killian picked Molly up in the carriage, and they drove to the park. The skies were threatening, so they decided to go back to the house. When they arrived, Thomas was sitting on the porch. "I'm glad you're here. I need to run down to the ironworks. I'll take your carriage in case it rains before I get back. Y'all wait here on the porch because Gretchen is off visiting her sister. I'll be back as soon as I can."

He got in the carriage and drove off.

Killian and Molly sat in the rockers and held hands as they chatted. As they sat, the sky got darker, and the clouds seemed to get lower. Soon it started sprinkling and that quickly turned into rain. The wind picked up and started blowing rain in on them, so they moved the chairs back. They sat down again, but a few minutes later, the wind picked up some more, and soon their backs were up against the wall. When they started getting wet, they jumped up and stood inside the door, watching for Thomas. But they couldn't see past the hitching post because of the hard rain.

Soon the rain was blowing sideways, and Killian had to get towels to put by the door so the rain wouldn't come under it. It didn't seem to be letting up, so they went into the parlor, and Killian built a fire in the fireplace because they were both damp. They sat down, and Killian got up every few minutes to see if he could see Thomas.

Killian finally looked back at her. "If he hasn't gotten here by now, then he is holed up somewhere. We'll just wait it out here."

He got a quilt and spread it on the floor in front of the fireplace. They sat down, and Molly smiled at him. "You know I am a ruined woman now."

"The only way to remedy that is for us to get married."

She looked surprised.

"Will you marry me?"

She sat there staring, and tears rolled slowly down her cheeks. Then a smile started to form, and she leaned over and wrapped her arms around his neck. They kissed so long that they had to come up for air.

"I will, Mr. O'Rourke. I will."

Killian reached into his back pocket and pulled out his grandmother's ring to show that Molly was spoken for. Her eyes got big, and then she started to cry. She put her arms around him and kissed him long and softly.

Killian reached in his pocket again. "Now, here's what the wedding ring looks like. I'll give it to you on our wedding day. Here's the one you'll give me," he said, pulling the other ring out of his other back pocket.

"Mrs. Molly McGuire O'Rourke. At least you can drop your middle name. I'm stuck with mine."

She laughed. "I like your middle name and everything about you."

The thunder started rumbling and rattling the windows. It got late, and they were still sitting on the quilt in front of the fireplace when Killian leaned over and kissed her. They both fell back. Killian rolled over, and his leg went between her legs.

She looked at him. "Think carefully about what you're going to do next because I'm not going to stop you." A tear rolled out of the corner of her eye.

Killian stopped and looked at her. He leaned down and kissed her, and then he removed his leg. They lay there holding each other. Killian woke up later, and the fire had died down. It was chilly. Molly was still asleep. He got up, picked her up, and laid her on the couch. He covered her up with the quilt and put wood on the fire. He decided to get into his bed in case Thomas came back while they were asleep.

Killian was dead asleep when a clap of thunder shook the whole house. He roused as the covers flew up, and he felt Molly jump in and grab him around the neck.

"Scared of a little thunder, little girl?"

"No," came the muffled voice under the covers. "I'm scared of the big thunder."

He laughed and held her. They both went back to sleep.

Killian was sleeping, and in a vision, he saw Thomas staggering across a field in the wind and rain. As Thomas got to the trees, a limb fell on top of him. Then he saw Thomas lying in his bed, and he watched him die. There was no pain.

Killian only heard quiet when he woke up. The storm was apparently over, so he jumped up, went to the front door, and looked out. Tree limbs and leaves covered the ground. There was no sign of Thomas.

Down the road, he saw some big limbs on the ground. The dream hit him. He went back to his bedroom and woke Molly up.

She smiled as she looked up. "I never knew it felt so good to sleep with someone's arms around you. I'm going to enjoy being married to you."

"Thomas hasn't come back yet. I saw a vision that a limb fell on him." He didn't tell her about the second part of the dream because he didn't want to believe it himself.

Killian and Molly ran out of the house, and that's when he saw Thomas's carriage and horse over at Patrick's. He ran over and saw that the left side of the carriage was damaged and the wheel was off. The horse looked as if it was about to drop. Killian unharnessed the animal and put it in the stall. He saddled up Thomas's horse and rode back to the house. "Get on," he said to Molly.

She jumped behind him with one leg on each side of the horse instead of sitting sidesaddle. That gave Killian the opportunity to ride faster. He trotted out and down the street. When he came to Molly's house, he turned and told her to check on her parents.

"But I want to go with you. Don't leave me."

He shook his head. "I may have to put Thomas on with me. Stay here. I'll be back."

"What do I tell my parents about where I've been?"

"Wait until I get back and I'll tell them, or you can tell them the truth. Start with sharing our wedding news. That should throw them off balance." He smiled and rode off.

233

Killian got to the main road and started to turn right for the ironworks. He had to ride around several downed trees. When he got to the road leading to the ironworks, he turned and saw the field that had been in his vision. He rode out across the field. He couldn't see any trees down, but something told him to keep riding. He finally came to a fallen tree and saw legs sticking out from under the branches. He jumped down and lifted up the branches. It was Thomas.

Killian looked him over and called his name. The old man opened his eyes. "Go get Killian, please," he said.

"Grandpa, it's me, Killian. Can you hear me?"

He picked up the limb and pushed until he got it off the old man. He helped him up and walked him over to the horse. He put Thomas's foot in the stirrup and pushed until he got him on. He swung up behind him and started home. He saw no blood or broken bones sticking out. He felt Thomas's chest and back, but felt no heat through the wet clothes. He reached up and felt his head. It felt warm. He rode along, holding Thomas's hand on him, and it got hotter and then started to cool down. He got Thomas home.

Patrick, Dean, and the other brothers saw him ride up, and they came running. They helped get Thomas off the horse and carried him inside. They took his wet clothes off, put a nightshirt on him, and put him in bed.

As Killian walked out on the porch, the third uncle, Dermit, looked at him. "If you hadn't been laid up with that damn woman and looked for Dad sooner, he might not be hurt."

234

Killian turned and hit Dermit as hard as he had ever hit anyone. Dermit hit the ground and was out cold. Someone grabbed Killian from the back, pinning his arms. The fourth uncle, Jeffrey, came at him, and Killian pushed back against whoever was holding him and kicked Jeffrey full in the face with both feet. Jeffrey's knees buckled, and he went down. When Killian's feet came down to the floor, he planted them, bent forward as far as he could, and threw the man off his back. That uncle hit his head on the arm of the rocking chair. He then hit the floor and didn't move either. Killian heard someone coming from the right and kicked in that direction, hitting someone's knee.

When Killian straightened up, someone hit him in the left side of his face. He felt as if he was floating until he hit the ground. Someone picked him up and held him while someone else hit him in the stomach and then in the face. It seemed to last forever.

The next thing he heard was Patrick and Dean screaming, "Get off of him! Leave him alone!"

They started throwing people to the ground.

Jeffrey stood up, barely conscious. "Dermit is right. Why didn't he go out and look for him sooner?"

Patrick asked Dermit, "Why didn't you go out and look for him in the storm?"

Jeffrey looked at Killian. "He was in the house with—"

"It don't matter what he was doing. Now anybody else who wants to fight, come up here and fight me," Patrick shouted."

Jeffrey collapsed again, unconscious.

235

Dean looked at them. "That goes for me too." There were only grandsons left standing. The four uncles were out cold.

Killian collapsed. Four people picked him up, carried him inside, and put him on his bed. He felt a cold rag on his face. His face, head, ribs, and stomach hurt. He opened his eyes and saw Linda's and Alberta's faces. As he came to, he could tell his eyes were swollen, and he wasn't sure if his ribs were broken.

Linda had a look of great concern on her face. "Can you look at Grandpa?"

Killian nodded, and they helped him up. They led him into Thomas's room. Several people were crowded around Thomas's bed.

Killian sat down by Thomas. "Patrick, get everybody out but you, Alberta, and Linda."

Brothers and grandchildren were protesting, but Patrick and Linda pushed them out the door. Killian went to Thomas and felt his head again. He moved his hands around and found a hot spot on the left temple. He held his hand there, and it got extremely hot—almost too hot to touch. It finally cooled down. He removed his hand, and there was a perfect handprint on Thomas's head.

Killian looked at Linda. "Wrap a bandage around his head until it goes away."

When Killian stood up, something hit him in the back. It was the floor.

He woke up and Patrick and Linda were there in his room. Patrick narrowed his eyes. "What were they talking about the girl being over here?"

"Thomas took our carriage before the storm. We were on the front porch. It rained so hard, we had to go in to keep from getting wet. We had nowhere else to go, so she slept on the couch, and I slept in my room. We had no choice. We had absolutely nowhere else to go."

Patrick nodded. "Is there anything else we should know?"

Killian opened his swollen eyes. "Yeah, I asked her to marry me."

Linda's eyes brightened. "Another wedding, I can't wait. When?"

Killian had passed out again. He was awakened by someone holding his hand and stroking his hair. He opened his eyes and looked at Molly. She was weeping.

"I'm all right, little girl. Don't cry."

She had tears dripping off her cheeks. "You look terrible."

He rose up with her help and looked in the mirror. Both eyes were black, and the left one was almost swollen shut. His lips were swollen and had dried blood on them. His ribs hurt.

"How's Thomas?"

"Come on. Let's go look. I want him to see you too."

Killian walked slowly, with one arm over Molly's shoulder and the other holding his ribs. They went into Thomas's room. Thomas was sitting up in bed, drinking coffee. He looked at Killian and almost screamed, "What the hell happened to you?"

Killian smiled as best he could. "I came off a horse. I'll be OK."

Patrick stood up from a chair against the wall. "Don't believe him. Dermit, Jeffrey, David, and Lonnie tried to kick the shit out of him and got it kicked out of themselves instead. All of them are still in bed recovering."

Thomas looked up at Patrick. "Paddy, as soon as they are all recovered, I want to see them all here before me."

Killian started to protest.

Thomas looked at Killian. "Nobody tells me what to do or not to do, and that includes you." He looked at Molly. "Put him to bed."

Molly led him out of Thomas's room and back to his room and pulled the covers down. Linda came in and took over. "Let me do that for you. You're not married to him yet."

Molly turned her back, and Linda pulled his pants and his shirt off and covered him up. His ribs were bruised badly.

Killian fell asleep immediately. Molly sat there by his side. He awoke about four hours later and looked up at Molly. "I'm sure you have better things to do besides sit here," he said.

"This is what I want to do and where I want to be. Can you understand that?"

He nodded. "I have two things I want to talk to you about. One is, make Thomas understand that it wasn't the beating that made me this weak. It was healing him that did it. I don't know what he's going to do to his four sons, but it wasn't all their doing. I've been beat worse than this by my brothers. OK? Make him or Patrick understand."

238

"The second thing I want to hear is how your parents took it when you told them you stayed all night and that I asked you to marry me."

Molly looked down. "Mother went crazy at first. She started screaming about how I was ruined and no man would want me now. She screamed at me until it made her sick and she went to bed. Father asked me what my side of the story was. I told him that Thomas took the horse and cart, and the storm hit so quick and so bad that I couldn't get home. He knows I don't like thunder and lightning, and he believed me. He asked me if you were in love with me, and I told him I was sure you were or you wouldn't have asked me to marry you. He smiled, kissed me, and said he always believed in me. He said he would deal with Mother.

"She finally came down and accepted the fact that I'm in love with you and am going to marry you. I asked to come back over here, and Father said OK, but I have to be home before dark. Dean is going to take me back."

"I'm glad to hear that. Let's make some wedding plans and get married as soon as we can. Is that OK with you?"

The tears started flowing again. "Get well, and we'll plan together."

When he woke up again, it was dark outside, and Molly was gone.

The next morning, when Killian opened his eyes, Thomas was sitting by his bed. He looked at the boy. "Molly told me what you said. Those boys will still have to answer to me. They don't pass judgment on anyone—you or that girl. It was my fault that that happened, and I've apologized to her and her father. He said he understood. Get well, boy, I need you."

239

Thomas left as Gretchen came in with some soup. He had a painful time sitting up to eat. His ribs still hurt, but they weren't broken.

After eating, he dozed off again. He was awakened by the sound of boots in the hall. He heard Patrick say, "Go on in there, and wives too."

It was quiet, and he heard Thomas clear his throat. "Let me tell you something. All of you better hear me because I'm only going to say this once. I had your wives come over to make sure you heard me. Some of you may still be addled from the whipping Killian put on you. If any of you ever touch my grandson again, or malign him or his fiancée, I will see that Patrick and Dean fire you from the jobs you have with me, and you'll move out of any property I own. Just nod if you get my meaning."

Killian didn't hear anything until Thomas said, "Now get out of my sight. All of you."

Chapter 13

Killian improved and was up and around in a week, if ever so gingerly because of his sore ribs. Thomas was improving, but Killian didn't like his color. Molly came over every day after school.

The second week, Patrick brought a new carriage home. Thomas and Killian took it out. Killian could feel every bump in the road in his rib cage. They were riding to the ironworks when Killian felt woozy. He grabbed Thomas's arm. Thomas stopped the carriage, and before he could speak, Killian had a vision and couldn't hear anything. Killian found himself looking down the street that Molly lived on. It was dark. He tried to look over at her house, but he was drawn to a house on the other side of the street. He went in, and there was a woman about fifty years old, lying dead. There was a lot of blood around her neck and head.

He heard something and listened. It was Thomas, and he was saying, "Killian, speak to me. Speak to me."

Killian opened his eyes and looked at Thomas. Thomas had tears in his eyes. "You took a harder beating than we thought."

Killian shook his head. "No, I had a vision." He told Thomas what he had seen.

Thomas looked off, thinking. "It hasn't happened yet, so we must be very careful."

He turned the carriage around, and they drove to Molly's street and turned around at the end. Killian pointed. "That house over there."

Thomas said, "We must drive over to the schoolhouse and ask Molly who lives there."

They pulled up at the schoolhouse, and Killian sat back in the seat to ease his ribs. "You'd better go ask her. The busybodies who watch the school will say something if I do it."

Thomas got out, and Molly met him on the porch. They talked. Killian had lain back and was resting with his eyes closed. When he opened them, he saw Thomas stopping Molly from coming out to him. Thomas turned and came back to the carriage.

He got back in the carriage. "Mrs. Matthews, recently a widow," he said. As he drove off, he added, "Molly said she would watch from her bedroom window tonight. I believe the same person is responsible for all of the murders, but that's just my hunch."

The next day, Molly came by before school. "Nothing last night, but I'll check again tonight," she said.

Killian looked at her. "You need to get your rest. You can't stay up all night and teach all day. Take care of yourself, please."

She smiled as she drove away.

The next day, Molly came riding up. "I sat up, and I heard a horse behind that house about one this morning, but I couldn't see behind the house."

Thomas nodded. "We'll check it out later on."

They were on the porch about ten thirty when they saw the sheriff ride by at a gallop, and the wagon went by a few minutes later. They knew that someone had found the dead woman. Killian felt drained and lay down to rest.

He heard Molly's voice. "Killian, are you OK?"

He opened his eyes, and Molly was standing there with her father. He started to get up, but she put her hand on his chest. "No, stay down. I just wanted to check on you, and Father was concerned about you also. Your swelling has gone down, and your black eyes have disappeared."

Killian asked, "How are you, Mr. McGuire? I have been meaning to come over to see you."

John smiled. "Don't get up, son. I just wanted to see you. I heard about your fight, and I understand you whipped four of your uncles."

"I'm not sure about who whipped who in that fight."

John laughed. "What did you want to see me about?"

"I would like to ask for your daughter's hand in marriage."

John cut his eyes over toward his daughter. "Well, I understand that you've already asked her."

"Yes, sir, but that was contingent on getting your permission. We wouldn't want to go against your wishes."

John laughed again. "Yes, you may marry my daughter, and you have my blessing."

"What about your wife, sir?"

"I've told her that if she wants to be a part of the inevitable, she'd better change her attitude. I think she's come around. I need to talk to your grandfather. Get well soon, son."

John went out on the porch, and they heard Thomas say, "Have a seat, John. Killian tells me your wife is concerned about Killian financially. She doesn't have to be. I'll provide for him long after I'm gone. I know a lot of people are saying that he doesn't work, but he's solved many problems at the ironworks and the mill. These were things that my sons couldn't solve on their own. He's wise beyond his years when it comes to business. Have you noticed the increase in production in the jobs room?"

"I certainly have. The word is, you put the fear of God into them."

"No. That was Killian's doing. He simply wrote in chalk what one shift did, and the second shift outdid them, then the third shift outdid the second. He didn't have to say a word to anybody. He wants to start at the bottom and work his way up, but I won't let him. He's done a lot of things like he did in your department. Of course, your promotion was all Paddy's doing."

John smiled. "I'm sure that will put my wife at ease, but the most important thing is for these two to love each other."

"Killian has told me he is in love with her. Of course, I knew it before he did." He laughed.

John laughed too. "I knew it too. I didn't know how long it was going to take them to realize it." They both laughed.

Killian smiled at Molly, and she bent down and kissed him.

He heard John say, "The thing that concerns me is these murders that are happening in our neck of the woods. I fear for my family. I may have to buy a handgun to carry."

"I have one I'll give you, but somebody has to find out who is doing this. I believe this to be the work of one man."

"Really? I haven't thought about that, but you must be right. Why do you think the sheriff can't find the killer?"

"Oh, I think he's doing the best he can. This person is smart, but he's bound to mess up sooner or later, and the sheriff will get him."

They went on talking, and Killian and Molly took the opportunity to practice their kissing. Molly sat back in her chair when Thomas came in to get one of the guns Killian had taken away from the two men on the trip with Alberta. He went back out, and Molly leaned back toward Killian.

Thomas and John came in and walked into Killian's room. John smiled at the two and said, "Well, have you two decided on when this wedding will take place?"

Molly smiled and said, "We both want it as soon as possible. I think it will depend on if Killian's father will come. He's already written him, and we should hear back from him soon."

John looked down at her. "When you find that out, get with your mother and plan it, and I'll pay for it." Thomas and John laughed.

Killian got a letter from his father saying that he wished he could be there for the wedding, but he couldn't afford to leave the farm, and his daughters-in-law wouldn't leave Ireland.

Killian was on the porch with Thomas when he received the news. "I have to go see Molly," he said.

The old man just nodded and said, "Before you go." He reached inside his shirt and pulled out a key on a piece of leather string. "If anything ever happens to me, come and get the trunk."

Killian nodded.

The wedding was planned for three weeks from then.

Those weeks were calm for Thomas and Killian. No visions, no murders, and no problems with the uncles. Killian's grandfather bought him a new suit and boots for the wedding. He had reservations in a hotel in Nashville for the honeymoon.

Chapter 14

One day, Killian sat on the porch while Thomas rode to the ironworks. He saw Alberta come out on her front porch for some air. He waved and went over to her house. He looked at her with a little embarrassment. "Can I ask you something personal? I probably should ask a man, but I don't know who to ask. I can talk to you and feel you will be honest with me."

She smiled. "If there's anything I can help you with, I'd be glad to do it."

He looked off into the trees, "Molly and I are both new at this marriage thing, and I wonder if there is any advice I can get about the wedding night. I mean, I know what to do, but neither one of us has done it before. I don't want to hurt her or appear stupid." He was red in the face and wouldn't look at her.

She smiled and took his hand. "Killian, you are very smart to seek this information before you marry. No man can tell you what a woman feels and expects. Only a woman who has been through it can do that. Will you let me go get Linda so we both can talk to you?"

He nodded, and she went next door and came back with Linda.

Linda put her hand on his shoulder. "Bertie told me what you wanted to know, and I think that's very considerate and sweet to think of you wife-to-be in that regard. We will be as factual as we can, so don't be embarrassed to ask questions."

They spent several hours talking to him. It was awkward at times, but it became less embarrassing. He felt surer about himself and about Molly.

Both women looked at him. "Encourage Molly to come talk to us." Linda looked at Alberta. "The worst advice I ever received about the wedding night was from my mother."

Alberta laughed. "Me, too. Why they do that, I don't know."

Killian shook his head. "Her mother, especially. The woman does not like me. I would expect her to give her advice that would ruin our wedding night."

Killian asked Molly to go over and talk with them. He told her they had requested the meeting. She was there for several hours also.

The wedding drew closer with no interference or visions.

Killian asked Thomas, "Would you stand up with me at the wedding?"

Thomas looked at him, and his eyes brimmed with tears. "You want me as your best man?"

Killian nodded. "You're the closest friend I have."

The old man looked away, unable to speak, and nodded.

The day of the wedding, Thomas came out completely shaven. He always seemed to have a two-day beard. He had on a black suit with shined boots. His gold watch chain was shining on his vest. They sat on the porch. Thomas looked over at him. "Killian, my time is near," he said.

Killian sat up. "No, it's not, or I would know." But he remembered his vision.

Thomas stared straight ahead. "You're too close to me to see this. I know it is near, and I want you to listen to me. You know you can't stop it. You can heal people, but you can't stop them from dying. It will be a while, so go ahead and get married and go on your honeymoon. I feel good knowing you have Molly to take care of you. I love you more than any of my sons or other grandchildren because you're special. I need to go to Molly's house and have a talk with her without you. I have to prepare her."

Thomas came back from Molly's, and he and Killian sat on the porch until it was time to go to the church. The wedding was going to be held at the big church in town because of the large number of guests who were invited.

Killian and Thomas arrived by carriage at the proper time. They went in the back and went to the groom's room, which doubled as a broom closet. It seemed like an eternity before the pastor said it was time. Killian and Thomas walked out front and stood, and the wedding march was played. The doors opened, and Molly walked in on her father's arm. Killian had never envisioned her as so beautiful. She had her mother's wedding dress on. It was a beautiful, white, floor-length dress. The top appeared to be made of diamonds because she sparkled with every step she took. The neckline was low, and Killian saw her cleavage for the first time. She wore a beautiful pearl necklace, and a veil over her head and face, but he could still see her beauty and her red hair. The train flowed behind her and dragged along the floor for six feet.

When she got up to the altar, they stopped, and the preacher looked up. "Who gives the woman to be wed?"

249

John seemed to swell with pride. He said, "I do," and he stepped back and offered her arm to Killian.

Killian took her arm, and he couldn't take his eyes off her.

The preacher said in a whisper, "Look at me for now, Killian." Killian smiled.

The ceremony went too long for Killian's taste, but the pastor finally pronounced them husband and wife. The preacher smiled. "You may kiss the bride."

Killian raised the veil and kissed Molly. He had never felt the softness of her lips as he did with that kiss. They walked down the aisle and into the basement for the reception. They stood in the receiving line with Thomas and Gretchen, Alberta and John and Mildred behind them. They shook hands with each guest. It seemed to take forever for the line to go down. Finally, the last three people were David McCall—which surprised everybody—Harmon Baker Drexler III, and his father. He knew they came to protect the bank's interests. Killian shook Harmon's hand.

When Killian clasped the father's hand, the vision of every woman who had been murdered flashed before his eyes. Killian couldn't breathe. He grabbed Thomas by his coat and motioned him over. They went into a side room, and Killian looked at him. "I know who murdered all those women. I saw the women dead as I shook his hand."

Thomas stood there silently.

"It's Mr. Drexler, senior," Killian said.

Thomas frowned. "How do we expose him without revealing yourself?"

250

Killian looked over to the corner of the room. "I will go to him alone and tell him I know it's him who murdered those women. If he denies it, then that might indicate he is innocent; but if he doesn't deny it, then he knows that I know, and he will be labeled as the killer. Then we'll see what he does."

Thomas nodded. "That should work. Go ahead, and I will watch."

About that time, Molly walked up. "What are you two doing?"

Thomas took her by the arm. "Come with me, and I'll tell you."

Killian walked over to Mr. Drexler and said, "May I have a word with you, sir?"

Drexler looked surprised. "Sure."

They stepped over to a corner, and Killian looked him in the eye. "I know it was you who murdered all those women. Right now, Grandpa and I are the only ones who know. Now, you do the right thing and you might spare your son, who is a suspect in the Townsend Road murder."

Drexler frowned. "How did you…know?"

"I didn't know for sure until you failed to deny it. That's what an innocent man would have done."

Killian stood there, and Mr. Drexler looked at him with fear in his eyes. Then he turned and walked out the door. Killian went back and joined Molly.

Molly leaned up to him. "Are you sure, Killian?"

He nodded.

After the reception, they changed their clothes, and Patrick and Linda drove them to the train station. They boarded the train and held hands for the four-hour ride to Nashville. When they arrived in Nashville, they went to the Maxwell House Hotel. With the advice Linda and Alberta had given them, they enjoyed the next three days and nights as much as any married couple ever had.

The fourth day, they were coming down from their room, when the clerk said, "Mr. O'Rourke, I have a telegram for you."

It read: "Killian. Stop. Thomas very ill. Stop. Come as quick as you can. Stop. Linda. Stop."

They ran back up to the room and packed. It was several hours before the train was scheduled to leave, but they finally boarded. The four-hour trip was agonizing. When they arrived back in Knoxville, the sheriff was at the depot, picking up supplies for the city. Killian asked him for a ride to the house.

"Sure, hop in. I'm ready to go."

On the way, the sheriff looked straight ahead. "Did you hear about old man Drexler at the bank?"

Killian shook his head.

"Took a gun and blew his own brains out. Left a note saying he was sorry for killing all those women. Can you believe that?"

Killian just shook his head. Molly gripped his hand tighter.

Killian ran into the house, followed by Molly. He went to Thomas's bed, where Thomas lay, looking gravely ill.

Patrick looked at Killian with tears in his eyes. "He's unconscious. He can't hear anyone anymore."

All his sons and grandchildren and daughters-in-law were crowded into the room.

Killian sat on the bed beside him. "Grandpa, it's Killian. Can you hear me?"

Patrick said, "The doctor says he's in a coma. He can't hear you."

The old man opened his eyes to the amazement of everyone, including the doctor, who was about to pronounce him dead. Thomas said in a weak voice, "What are you doing here?"

Patrick looked over Killian's shoulder. "He told us not to send for you. I don't know who did, but now that you're here, do something."

Everyone looked confused, especially the doctor.

Killian leaned toward Thomas. "Grandpa, you're going to have a good journey. There will be no pain."

His grandfather smiled at him. "You saw? No pain?"

Killian nodded. "I saw. There will be no pain. You can go now."

Thomas closed his eyes and slipped away.

Patrick screamed, "Do something! Damn you, do something!"

Killian turned and looked at Patrick with tears in his eyes. "There's nothing to do. He's gone. I have no power to stop him." Tears streamed down his face.

Dean looked at Patrick. "What makes you think he could do anything?"

Patrick looked at Killian. "I don't understand why you didn't do anything to save him, but understand this: be moved out of this house by tomorrow."

Killian stood up and faced Patrick. "Let's get him buried before you start fighting over his scraps."

Everybody came by for a last look, and since Patrick was first, he was the first to walk out.

Killian met him on the porch. "Patrick, I can't stop death. That's one thing I cannot do. That's why he told you not to contact me. He didn't want me exposed to the rest of the family, like you just did."

Patrick looked out into the dark. "It sounded like you knew he was going to die."

"I did. He told me before I left, but he told me it wouldn't be before I got back. I think he had planned for me to be gone when it happened so those who know wouldn't want me to try to save him. I did have a vision that he would die peacefully, but I didn't know when. He must have had something wrong with him, because he knew his time was limited. Do you understand?"

Patrick nodded. "I'm sorry for what I said about you moving out. You do know that this house is rightfully mine."

Killian looked at him. "I have no problem with that. I'll make arrangements."

Patrick sat on the porch with his eyes and ears burning. He was confused. The undertaker soon arrived.

The day of the funeral, Killian felt the hatred of almost everybody except Linda and Alberta. He wasn't sure how Patrick and Dean felt.

The day after the funeral, Killian received a message to come to the office of Thomas's friend and attorney, Mr. Fehy O'Hara. When he arrived, he saw all six of his uncles sitting there.

Fehy nodded at him. "I am to read the last will and testament of Thomas O'Rourke. 'I, Thomas O'Rourke, being of sound mind and body, leave all my money and real property, to include my house, businesses, and investments, to my grandson, Killian G. O'Rourke. In the event Killian does not survive, everything goes to the Widows and Orphans Fund in Knoxville.'"

Fehy looked up. "Are there any questions?"

They all looked at Killian, and he had his mouth open. He closed it and frowned. "Surely, he didn't do that."

Fehy nodded. "You can do anything you want with it, but it's yours."

Dermit stood up and looked at his nephew. "Oh, you act like you knew nothing of it?"

Fehy interjected. "He didn't. Thomas told me to not tell Killian until this meeting with you."

Dean almost screamed, "Where does that leave us?"

Killian stood up and looked at his six uncles. "Right where you've always been. You'll remain in the same jobs and the same houses and receive the same pay as always. In the meantime, you better make damn sure I stay alive."

He got up and walked out.

The End